CASSIE LOVES BEETHOVEN
Alan Arkin

Illustrations by Hala Wittwer

HYPERION BOOKS FOR CHILDREN
NEW YORK

For the people of Cape Breton Island

CHAPTER 1

"**W**E NEED A COW," Hallie said one night as she was serving dinner.

"Whatever for?" her father, Myles, asked, breaking off a piece of homemade bread and biting off a huge piece. "Don't we have enough to do as it is?"

"They're no work, they look after themselves," Hallie's brother, David, said unintelligibly, shoveling soup into his mouth as fast as he could get it in.

"Nothing looks after itself," said Myles.

"Well, cows come close," Hallie said, sitting down at the table. "You don't have to brush them, you don't have to walk them, you don't have to buy special food. . . ."

"Where would it stay?" Myles asked.

"We have a bigger place than the Donovans," said David, "and they have two cows."

"Plus," Hallie added, holding her right index finger tightly against the left, "we would have our own milk, our own yogurt, our own butter, our own cheese, and I could sell what's left, *plus,"* she added loudly with a long pause for effect, "our own *ice cream.*"

"You talked me into it," said Myles, and he held up his own finger. *"Provided . . ."* he said, waiting for Hallie to finish the thought.

". . . we take care of it," Hallie and David said together, and that was that.

You'd think the last thing in the world the Kennedys needed was a cow. It wasn't as if they didn't have enough to do already. There was the store to run, a hundred-year-old house to look after, school for Hallie and David, and all the cooking and cleaning and gardening. The cow would be a big new responsibility for them, Myles thought, but he knew his children and what they were capable of. Hallie was thirteen and David only ten, but when they said they could do something, they did it.

Also, in Margaree, where the Kennedys lived, on the western side of the island, there wasn't much in the way of diversion. The nearest mall or movie theater was ninety miles away, so the people of Margaree are used to making their own entertainment.

The cow would be work, thought Myles, but it would also be fun for Hallie and David. Their mother had died four years earlier, and since that time Myles had promised himself he'd try to indulge them whenever he could. This seemed to be one of those times. So Myles gave in to their idea and found, before long, that he, too, was looking forward to having a cow around to brighten up the property.

During the next few weeks, whenever they had time off, the three of them worked on building a sturdy shed in back of the house and ran a barbed-wire fence around a big piece of the yard. In the evenings, after the chores were done, they went through the local newspapers to see if any livestock was being advertised. It wasn't long before they found something that looked promising. A farmer in Port Hawkesbury was selling his stock and retiring to the mainland.

Hallie called the number in the paper, and spoke to the farmer. "Yes," he said, "I have a couple of bulls and a dozen cows for sale."

"We only want one cow," said Hallie.

"Well," said the farmer, "I've been hoping to sell all of them at once, but I'm not having any luck. Why don't you come on down and have a look? If you find something you like I'll drive the cow back to your place in my rig." Hallie checked with her father—he said it sounded good, and they made plans to go see the farmer on the weekend.

That Saturday Myles and Hallie and David drove to Port Hawkesbury to look at the cows. It was a two-hour trip and most of the way down they talked about dairy farming, a subject they knew almost nothing about. They speculated on the wonders of cud. They tried to figure out how cheese was made. They counted up how many flavors of ice cream existed in the world, whether or not cows could become pets, and the various color combinations cows came in.

"We should look for an orange cow," David said with authority.

"Why?" asked Hallie.

"They have the best temperament," said David.

"Who told you that?" Hallie asked, not believing him for a moment.

"Orange animals have the best disposition."

"Since when?"

"It's the truth."

"Since when?"

"Golden retrievers. Orange cats. They have the best temperaments."

"What about orange-utans?" Hallie asked.

"I'm serious," said David.

"So am I," said Hallie.

"I don't know about orange-utans," said David.

When they reached Port Hawkesbury they followed the farmer's directions ("Left at the second gas station, right at the blue cottage with the broken white shutters") and were soon at the farm. The farmer, who'd been waiting for them, took them inside to meet his family and made them some tea. They talked about the weather for a while, then the farmer took them out to his barn. He introduced them to the cows, and then left them alone to look over the livestock and make up their minds. The cows were all clean and they looked well fed and even happy, if you can tell such things with cows, but David seemed slightly disappointed.

"What's wrong?" Hallie asked him, when the farmer was out of earshot.

"I was hoping for an Oreo cow," David said stoically.

"A what?" Hallie asked, crinkling up her nose.

"An Oreo cow, like the kind we saw in Maine that time. The ones with the black front and the black rear and the big white stripe around the middle."

"'Oreo' is not what they're called," said Hallie.

"It's what they look like."

"But it's not what they are," said Hallie.

"What are they, then?" David asked.

"I don't remember," said Hallie.

"Belted Gallaways," Myles said.

"To me they will always be Oreos," said David.

"Well, you'd better make your pick from this batch," said Myles. "We're lucky to find anything at these prices."

Before long they narrowed their choice down to a young tan-and-white Guernsey. "A good choice," said the farmer, "she's already giving plenty of milk."

"She also seems the most intelligent," said David.

"Milk is what we're after," said Hallie, "not conversation."

So the deal was done. Myles gave the farmer a deposit and they left, with the farmer promising to see them the following Saturday.

Saturday came. The electric fence was up, the shed was built, and at four o'clock the farmer arrived with his rig. He backed up behind the house, swung down the hatch on the truck, and opened the fence. All four of them pulled and pushed the cow until she reluctantly backed out of the truck. With her back legs she stepped gingerly off the metal ramp, mooed dramatically, and pawed nervously as she dropped down to the soft earth below.

"She's not temperamental," the farmer said, trying to reassure everyone. "She just don't like to walk backward. They're all like that."

Once out of the truck the cow did seem more relaxed, and when her breathing slowed down they gently walked her into the large enclosure. They shut the gate on her new home and paid the farmer. He started to leave.

"What's her name?" David called out. "Does she have a name?"

"We been calling her Cassie," the farmer said, "not that it makes much difference." He hopped into the cab and started the engine. "Let me know how you're doing," he called as he drove off.

"What did he mean, 'not that it makes much difference'?" David asked with a suspicious frown, once the truck was out of sight.

"He meant she wouldn't know her name," said Hallie.

"Why not?" David asked indignantly.

"Cows don't tend to be too smart," said Hallie. "They're not like dogs. They don't come when they're called. They don't do anything interesting."

"Maybe this one will," said David.

"Maybe she'll come when she hears a food bell, but that's about all," said Hallie.

"Well, that would be a start," David said hopefully. "If she can tell what a food bell means, we could probably train her to come when she hears her name."

"How would we do that?" Hallie asked.

"Easy," said David. "You call her name and ring the food bell at the same time for a couple of weeks. Then you just stop ringing the bell."

"It sounds good in theory," said Hallie.

Myles and David joined Hallie on the fence and examined the new member of the family. The cow busied itself, sniffing around the ground and getting used to its new surroundings.

"Here, Cassie!" David called out.

The cow didn't move. She didn't look up. "Here, Cassie!" He called again, louder this time. There was still no response.

"You try," David said to Hallie, eager for them to begin a personal relationship with the new member of the family.

Hallie called her name, but she, too, got no response.

David picked a clump of long grass and held it out to the cow, calling her at the same time. Still nothing happened.

"It might take a while," said Myles.

"If it works at all," said Hallie.

"If she doesn't answer to Cassie we could give her a new name," said David.

"What for?" Hallie asked.

"Well, she's our cow, we should get to call her whatever we want."

"How about 'Cassandra,'" said Hallie.

"No good," said David.

"What's wrong with it?"

"I don't like it when people give animals fancy names," said David. "I think they do it to make the animals look stupid."

"But that's her name," said Hallie.

"No, it's not," said David. "Her name's Cassie."

"Cassie's short for Cassandra."

"Oh," said David.

"Got any other ideas?" Hallie asked.

"Well, maybe we should just call her Cassie for a few days and see if we like it."

For the next few days David and Hallie thought about her name. They rolled it around in their mouths, they called it out to her, and before long they just forgot about any other possibility. Her name was Cassie, and that was that.

CHAPTER II

THE NEW COW MEANT new expenses. To help pay for her, David and Hallie had to dip into their savings. They also had to put in longer hours working at the store. The store was just down the road from the house. Second Time Around, it was called, and it sold a great jumble of things, mostly old, some nearly antiques, and some just worn out, but it attracted the tourists, and it kept Myles out of the mines and the fishery, so it suited him just fine. Hallie and David went there each day after school and looked after customers while Myles drove around the island looking for old farm furniture and knickknacks. Between customers they did their homework.

Most secondhand store owners put codes on their price tags, so they can remember how much they paid for the items they sell, but Myles never got around to doing that.

Hallie made up outrageous prices and bargained with people.

David just took whatever the customer offered, which drove Hallie crazy.

"David practically gives everything away," she scolded Myles, whenever he came back from one of his trips. "You have to put prices on things."

"Well, you always get more than the stuff is worth, so it pretty much evens out, doesn't it?"

"I'm the only practical member of the family," she groused, picking up a dustcloth and attacking an old bureau with it. "Everyone has their head in the clouds. They forget that we have to eat and pay bills."

David seemed amused at the idea.

"You have to take more of an interest in this," she

said in her most no-nonsense tone. "This is serious."

"It's not that serious," said David.

"It *is* serious," said Hallie. "It's *very* serious. It's business!"

David wrinkled up his nose. "That's right," he said. "Business. BUSY-NESS. Stuff to keep you *busy*. That's what the word means."

"This business is what allows us to live, you know," Hallie said, trying to be parentlike.

"We'll always be able to live," David answered.

"Not if we don't work, we won't," said Hallie. "Who'll pay for the mortgage on the house?"

"We could live in a tent."

"Where?" Hallie asked. "In the woods?"

"In somebody's backyard," said David.

"What would we do for food?"

"If we were starving, friends would take pity on us," said David.

"Don't you have any pride?" Hallie asked.

David shook his head no.

There were no customers, so they closed the store, and just as they did every day, they stopped at some open fields before going home. They picked aromatic clumps of grass and wildflowers to bring back to Cassie. And this day, for the first time, Cassie trotted over to the fence when she saw the two of them reach the mailbox.

"See that?" said David. "She knows us. She's smarter than you think."

"She's a genius," said Hallie.

"Well, it's a start, isn't it?"

"I don't know what it is," said Hallie, not wanting to let David win the point. But in the stillness of the evening she had to admit the cow had a calming influence on the place. She found herself musing when she watched Cassie. Daydreaming. Which wasn't like her. Cassie was a welcome addition, no doubt about it.

But there was no milk. Not a drop.

They'd all seen farmers milking their cows, so they had an idea of how it was done, but as much as they coaxed, as much as they pulled and poked, nothing happened.

"We'd better call the farmer and let him know something's up," Myles said one evening, tired of staring into an empty milk pail. "It's been three weeks and we haven't seen any action."

He went to the house and called the farmer. "Mr. Murdoch," he said, "I'm concerned that Cassie might not be a qualified milker."

"Oh, I don't think that's possible," the farmer said. "I milked her myself the morning she left here."

"She's not giving us anything over here," said Myles.

"Have you ever been around a cow?" Murdoch asked.

"Not since I was a kid," said Myles.

"Maybe you haven't got the touch," said the farmer.

"Maybe not," said Myles, not pleased with Murdoch's slighting of his abilities. How hard is it to milk a cow, after all?

"Well, if you're having a problem I'll gladly take her back in exchange for one of the others," Mr. Murdoch said.

"We'll think about it," said Myles.

"We're not giving her back," David said fiercely.

"I just said we'll think about it," said Myles.

"We don't want another cow," David said, "and anyway, how big a problem can it be? She shoves the stuff in, all we have to do is get it out."

"What's Murdoch got that we haven't got,

anyway?" Hallie asked.

"Beats me," said Myles.

Later that morning Myles had a talk with the vet.

"It's probably nothing serious," the vet said. "I'll come over this afternoon and have a look-see." Later that day the vet came by and examined Cassie. He checked her eyes, her tongue, her nose, her udders, her feet; he felt her stomach and he even examined some of her droppings. He walked around the cow a couple of times, squatted on the ground, and pulled on his lower lip.

"What do you think it is, Casper?" Myles asked.

"Can't tell," said the vet, frowning. "She's a fine-looking cow. I don't know what it is."

"Could she be sick?" asked David.

"She looks healthy to me," said Casper. "If she was sick we'd see it in her behavior. She'd be off her feed, or there'd be some indication somewhere in her body. But her eyes are clear, her stomach isn't bloated, there's no sign of infection in her udders, her tongue's a good color and uncoated, so I don't know what it is."

"Could it be her diet?" Hallie asked.

"Could be," said the vet. "Could be anything."

"Should we change what she eats?" asked Myles.

"It couldn't hurt," said the vet. "We could try some of the alfalfa or rye grass we have on my place, and see what that does."

"What about vitamins?" asked David.

"You could try that, too," said the vet. "I can give you some samples and we can see how she does on them. If all else fails, we can put her on hormone treatments or antibiotics."

Myles stiffened. "I'd like to try to avoid that," he said.

"I don't blame you," said the vet quickly. "I was thinking, as a last resort."

"Well, I'd like to come up with something else first, if we can," said Myles.

Puzzled, they all stood looking at Cassie, who seemed completely content and comfortable and certainly beautiful.

The vet got up and slapped his old straw hat onto his head. "Well," he said, "we'll work our way through the list of possibilities and see if we come up with an answer. Whatever it is, I don't think it's very serious." He rumpled David's hair, said good-bye, and drove off in his truck.

Myles tried not to show it, but it was frustrating news. Now they were stuck with veterinarian bills. If the grasses from the vet's place didn't work, they would have to lay out more for special foods, additives, vitamins, and who knew what else.

For the next few weeks they brought in different kinds of grass and hay, some of which they scythed themselves from the vet's fields. Cassie ate it all, chomping away at whatever was in front of her, but nothing happened. Next, they consulted with companies that specialized in animal vitamins. They tried everything that was recommended and nothing worked. There seemed to be nothing left to try except antibiotics, which Myles was dead set against.

"It'll get into the milk," he said, "and then we'll be drinking antibiotics. I don't want that to happen."

Antibiotics were not the solution. Myles was sure of that, but he was beginning to get impatient with the situation. Hallie and David weren't up to handling all the problems without him and he was swamped with work. Things in the store needed his attention and with summer coming there were estate sales all over the island. He didn't have time to worry about the cow. Myles tried not to show his frustration, but it was getting to be too much for him.

One day, after a frustrating talk with a vitamin salesman, he threw up his hands. "That's it," he said. "I'm done. We don't have a milk cow. We have a thousand-pound pet. Except she's not housebroken and she doesn't do tricks." Myles left the house, went down to the store, and began hammering on things.

Hallie and David went outside and sat hunched behind the house, chewing furiously on long pieces of grass while they scrutinized the cow.

"It just doesn't make sense to have a pet cow," said Hallie.

"We're not giving her back," said David, looking steely-eyed, his jaw set.

"We bought her for the milk. To save us some money and maybe make a little," Hallie said. "She's not a pet."

"She is."

"No, she's not."

"I love her."

"How can you love her? She's just like any other cow. She stands there and chews her cud. She doesn't even know you."

"She does," said David. "She's not a car, you know, she has a brain and feelings just like the rest of us."

"Maybe so, and maybe not," Hallie said.

"She's not going anywhere," said David, not interested in any of Hallie's opinions. "If she goes, I go."

"That's a little dramatic," said Hallie.

"Well, it's the way I feel."

"But we got her because we thought she'd have some use," Hallie said in her most practical tone. "I feel like she's here under false pretenses."

"She's not doing it on purpose," said David.

Hallie didn't like feeling guilty and heartless, but she was beginning to, in spite of herself. David's feelings for the cow were intimidating her. And, after all, the cow had been her idea to begin with. They sat silently, both fixed on the real problem they were dealing with. Suddenly David got up and started walking toward the road.

"Where are you going?" Hallie called out.

"I'm going to see Vivian Keats," David said over his

shoulder. "She'll know what to do."

"She doesn't know anything about cows," Hallie said with a snort.

"She knows a lot of surprising things," David said.

"We're not going to do any psychic healing on the cow!" Hallie called out.

"You have to try to keep an open mind about things," David answered.

"Be back by six!" Hallie shouted and she went into the house to begin dinner.

CHAPTER III

B Y CAPE BRETON STANDARDS, Vivian
Keats was an odd bird. She was a librarian from
the States who had retired early and bought a small
place in Margaree Harbour. She spent her time paint-
ing landscapes and improving everyone's mind.
During the warm weather she traipsed through the vil-
lage with a floppy hat and sandals and a folding chair
and an easel looking for old boats with barnacles and

fishermen scraping them. While she painted she told the fishermen endless stories about the history of the island and where they all came from. The fishermen smiled and waved and laughed in all the right places, but paid no attention to her at all.

When David had free time he went to Vivian's and painted along with her. He liked the fact that she was a character, and listened wide-eyed as she lectured about things no one else on the island seemed to know. Or care about. He didn't think he was a very good painter, but he had a good time. Every time he made a brush stroke Vivian shouted "Great! Wonderful!" and then she'd explain the hidden meaning behind each of his colors. "Every color signifies a different emotion," she'd tell him. "Mix the wrong colors together and you can actually make people sick." Her lectures didn't stop her from trying any color combinations that came into her head.

When David got to Vivian's he found her in the garden talking to her tomatoes.

"Hello, you beautiful thing," she was saying to one of them. "Yes, you are beautiful, and you know it, too, don't you?" David sat near her and listened patiently as she went on. He'd seen her talk to her vegetables before and it didn't faze him. She worked the dirt around the plants and as she did she spoke to each one. "You're not looking as good as your sisters over here, are you? What's wrong? Aren't you getting enough attention?" she said, listening for an answer. After a while she got up. "Well, that's enough of that. How are you, David?" she said. "What's going on in your life?"

David sat down and told her about their problems with Cassie and all the things they'd tried.

"Perhaps we should do a psychic healing on your cow," Vivian said, wiping the dirt off her hands. She stood up and headed for the house.

"I don't think my Dad would go for that," said David.

"It's not very complicated," Vivian explained. "You just put your hands on her and stand in silence for a while."

"It's not his kind of thing," David said.

"I could show him an article that proves it works."

"He probably wouldn't read it."

"What a shame," said Vivian. "There are so many

things going on in the world, I'd hate to be left out. Well, maybe we can find something on the Internet that's a little more conventional," she said, and turned on the computer. "So many wonderful things going on in the world," she said. "So many changes. You'd think everyone would want to be in on it, wouldn't you?"

"Maybe some people like things the way they are," said David.

"But it doesn't work that way," said Vivian. "Nothing stays the same. Everything changes."

"I guess some people want things to change slowly," said David.

"Maybe so," said Vivian, and for the rest of the afternoon they drank tea, talked philosophy, and searched for a way that would coax Cassie into becoming a milk cow.

That night David came back from Vivian's late, as usual. Hallie and Myles were almost through with dinner.

"Well," said Myles, munching on a carrot, "what are we doing wrong?"

"Nothing *wrong*," said David with authority, "but there are other things to do."

"Like what?" Myles asked suspiciously, waiting for some strange Vivian idea to come from David.

"Vivian thinks we should play music for Cassie," David said breezily, helping himself to some chicken and mashed potatoes.

"Serenade her?" Myles asked, picking chicken out of his teeth.

"I think so," said David. "She went on the Internet. She looked up 'cows' and found articles about the effects of music on animals, and that it's a scientifically proven fact that it calms them down and makes them happy. It also makes them give more milk."

"Cassie doesn't give *any* milk," said Myles, "and she is calm enough already."

"Maybe she's not," said David.

"Look at her," said Myles. "She's a calm cow."

"Maybe she's churned up inside."

"I'm not going to serenade the cow," said Myles.

"Why not?" Hallie asked. "Don't you love Cassie?"

"I'm not going to serenade any cows," Myles repeated. "It's your idea. If you think it's going to work, you go out and sing to her."

"I can't carry a tune," said Hallie. "I would if I could."

"Vivian says that there have been many studies about playing music for animals," David said, pouring too much gravy on his potatoes. "She said they get happier and give more milk if you play music for them."

"*Play* music for them," said Hallie with relief. "That doesn't mean we have to stay up all night and sing to her, does it, now?"

"I don't think so," said David. "Maybe we could put a radio in there."

"Well, that's a different story," said Myles. "We can give that a try. At least it will be cheaper than the vitamins."

After dinner they walked down to the store, rummaged through the attic and came up with an old tube radio that was covered with dust and cobwebs. They cleaned it up, found an extension cord, plugged it in in the kitchen and ran it down to Cassie's shed. Myles turned the dial to one of the three stations they could get in Margaree. It was playing Irish jigs. The next station had news and weather and the last one had a woman reading mournful poetry about drowning sailors. "I guess it's the jigs," said Myles.

"That doesn't seem right," said David.

"Why not?" Myles asked.

"I don't know," said David. "But if I was a cow I don't think Irish jigs would inspire me."

"Let's give it a try anyway," said Hallie. "Music is music."

They left the radio on and went about their business, but the Irish jigs soon stopped and were replaced by a live rock concert coming from somewhere across the island. They heard it blaring all the way from the house. "Hmmm," said Hallie. "What do you think? Should we change the station?"

"I thought you said music is music," Myles said.

"I guess I did," Hallie said, "but if you were a cow, would this make *you* want to give milk?"

"Well . . ." said Myles, pulling on his mustache, "if this is going to be a scientific experiment, we'd better try some other method, because you never know what they're going to play on the local radio. I'll make the supreme sacrifice."

Myles went to his bedroom and brought down the old and precious Grundig shortwave radio that someone had traded for a desk a few years earlier. He put the radio on the roof of the shed and covered it with a piece of plastic to protect it from the elements.

The Grundig picked up stations hundreds of miles away. Myles turned the dial and stopped at a station that played golden oldies twenty-four hours a day. They listened for a while to make sure the station was trustworthy, and then went back in the house for the night. The next morning Hallie and David got up early to see Cassie. The radio was still going, still playing the same kind of music. They examined Cassie, who seemed calm, cool, and collected—not much different from the night before.

"Let's give her a try," said David. Hallie rubbed her hands together, knelt down, grabbed a teat, took a deep breath, and gave a tug. A streak of milk squirted into the dirt.

"Wow!" said David. "Did you see that? It worked!"

"Go get a pail!" Hallie said excitedly.

David ran into the house and got a washbasin. He ran back out and put it under Cassie's udder. Hallie pulled again. Nothing. She pulled again harder, but still nothing came out.

"Well, *something* happened, that we know," David said in triumph. "The music worked!"

"One squirt doesn't prove anything," said Hallie. She folded her arms and sat back in the hay.

"Milk is milk, isn't it?" David asked indignantly.

"One drop?" Hallie said sarcastically. "It could be just a fluke."

"We have to keep trying," said David. "We should probably try other kinds of music, too."

"Probably the calmest music would make her the calmest," said Hallie.

"That makes sense," said David, "the calmer and happier she is, the more milk she'll probably give."

"How do we find calm music?" asked Hallie.

"Vivian," said David.

Hallie mulled it over. "Well," she said bravely, "this is science."

David came back late for dinner again, but this time Hallie and Myles were looking forward to the news.

"Well?" Hallie asked, as soon as David walked in the door.

"Classical music, not popular," said David.

"Why's that?" Myles asked.

"Vivian said popular music was basically for dancing and sooner or later it would make Cassie jumpy."

"So what do we do?" Myles asked.

"We try to find a classical station on the radio."

They finished dinner, went out to the radio and turned the dial until they came to a station that was playing something serious and important and slightly boring.

"This must be it," said David.

They listened for a few minutes, then left Cassie with her music. Every hour or so they came back to the shed to see if the music was the same, and it was. After the first night, they knew they had the right station. The announcers were as serious as the music. The music they introduced had all been written by people with unpronounceable names, and the pieces all had numbers.

The next morning they went out to see if there were any results. Hallie sat down by Cassie's side again, pulled, and sure enough, there was another squirt of milk. "I think we're on the right track," she said.

They continued playing the classical music day and night for several weeks. They even started getting used to it, and almost began enjoying it, although they weren't ready to admit it. A couple of the names of the composers even began sounding familiar. One day David even figured out what a concerto was.

"A concerto is when you hear one instrument more than all the others. It's like one piano or one violin is having an argument with the whole orchestra and for a while it looks like the one instrument is winning, then the orchestra wins for a while, but in the end they all come to an agreement."

And Cassie began to give milk. For a few days it was just a squirt or two, but then it was a cup, then a quart, then several gallons a day. They had enough for their own needs and soon they had some to share with neighbors.

It was then that the strange thing occurred.

CHAPTER IV

THAT SATURDAY MORNING David went out to milk Cassie. When he came back he had a peculiar look on his face. Hallie was out somewhere and Myles was drinking his coffee and reading the paper. David sat down at the kitchen table. He stared straight ahead, focusing on nothing in the room.

"No milk today?" Myles asked, without looking up from his paper.

"I can't tell," David said.

"Why not?" Myles asked.

"Cassie won't stand up."

"She won't stand up? Why won't she stand up?"

"She said she's not in the mood."

"She's not in the mood? Why does she have to be in the mood?" Myles asked.

"She told me she just heard the most beautiful piece of music in the whole world, and it disturbed her emotionally. She needs to rest."

"Cassie told you this?" Myles asked.

"Yes."

Myles pulled on his mustache and slowly nodded his head a few times. "Was that the only thing she said, or did she have other things on her mind?"

"She did have other things on her mind," said David.

"Such as?"

"She wants to know what the music was."

Myles looked at him skeptically.

"Maybe you should come outside," David said. "I don't know how to deal with this."

Myles put the paper down, hitched up his pants,

and went out back with David. Cassie was lying down facing away from them, breathing hard and moaning softly.

"Hello, Cassie," David said in a respectful whisper.

Cassie turned her head toward David and sighed a long, deep sigh. "I can't make small talk right now," she said.

David looked at his father. His father looked at him.

"Is there something troubling you?" David asked.

"Yes, there is," said Cassie wistfully. "The music I just heard has torn me apart. I don't know what's happened to me."

Myles turned pale and coughed into his fist.

"I'm sorry if the music upset you," David said quietly. "We thought it was making you happy."

"Oh, my," said Cassie. "It has made me happy. It's made me happier than I thought possible in this life. It's brought me to places that I didn't know existed. But this last piece . . . the piece they just played . . . it made me . . ." She struggled for the words. ". . . almost *too* happy. . . . It made me yearn for things and places that perhaps don't exist in this world."

"We're very, very sorry if it disturbed you," David said quietly and respectfully.

"Well, yes, it did disturb me," said Cassie, "but with dreams of something beautiful and very grand. I think it may not be a bad thing to be disturbed in that way. I feel my heart ripping open, but perhaps it is only stretching to have room for more beautiful things."

"That's a nice way to look at it," said David. "Very nice. Isn't it, Dad?"

"Yes," said Myles, in a strange and muffled voice, "a very nice way to look at it."

Cassie started to say something, then stopped herself.

"What is it?" David asked gently.

"You are all very kind to me. You feed me, give me shelter, and I am grateful for your generosity. If what I'm about to ask is an imposition, I beg you to tell me." She hesitated.

"What is it?" David asked.

"Do you suppose there is a way that I could hear that music again? It would mean a great deal to me. I need to know how sounds coming from a small wooden box can affect me in such a profound way."

"We'll see what we can do," said Myles.

"Thank you," Cassie said quietly, elegantly, lowering her eyes.

"I'll get right on it," Myles said, relieved to have a reason to leave. He hurried into the kitchen and plunked himself down at the table. Just then, Hallie came home from an errand in town.

"Good morning, Dad," she said.

"Go and say hello to your cow," Myles said softly.

"Excuse me?" Hallie asked.

"Go and say hello to your cow," Myles repeated. He sometimes had a tone in his voice that people listened to without questioning. This was one of those times.

Hallie examined her father for a hint of what was behind the tone, but she couldn't read anything in his face. She put her bags down on the table and went to the yard.

Myles sat in the kitchen and listened to the hum of the refrigerator.

A few minutes later Hallie and David came back in. They sat at the table and joined their father in silence.

Myles got a homemade pie and a pitcher of milk. He set out plates and forks and glasses and the three of them concentrated on the tangible and comfortable act of eating dessert.

"She wants to hear that same music again," said David after a while.

"Do we know what it was?" Hallie asked.

"No," said David.

"How do we find out?" asked Hallie.

"I guess we call the radio station," said Myles, his mouth full of pie. "They must keep a log of everything they play. If we tell them what time it was on, maybe they'll tell us what it was." They sat silently again, eating furiously to keep their minds from spinning off.

"What do we do?" Hallie asked, spooning up pie as fast as she could get it into her mouth.

"About what?" Myles said, getting more milk from the fridge.

"We have a cow that talks."

"Well . . ." said Myles, taking another huge bite, "there's nothing to do. We just try to find the music she wants to hear."

"We have a talking cow," said Hallie.

"Let's just take it one step at a time," said Myles softly.

After her pie, Hallie went back outside and got the number of the station from the dial on the radio. She tried looking it up in the phone book, but the phone book didn't list stations by number, just by name. "Well," she said, "I don't know how to find the phone number of the station."

"Vivian will know," said David, starting for the phone.

"I'll call her," said Hallie. "I might as well get used to it. I have a feeling we'll be seeing a lot more of her." She picked up the phone and dialed Vivian's number.

"Good morning, whoever it is!" Vivian chirped.

"Hello, Mrs. Keats," Hallie said, wincing just a little at Vivian's high-pitched exuberance. "This is Hallie Kennedy. Could I ask you a question?"

"Shoot!" said Vivian.

"How do you find the phone number of a radio station?"

"What's the station, Hallie?" Vivian asked.

Hallie looked at the paper in her hand. "Eleven-eighty," she said.

"Are you listening on your shortwave?"

"Yes," said Hallie.

"Then it's WQXR in New York City. If you wait a minute I'll get you their phone number."

Why on earth would Mrs. Keats have the phone number of WQXR? Hallie wondered. How many times in one lifetime do you need to call a radio station in New York?

"Here it is," Vivian said. She gave Hallie the number. "That's a U.S. area code," she added.

"I know," said Hallie a little curtly. She thanked Vivian, hung up, and dialed the radio station.

A man answered.

Hallie asked the man if he could tell her what they'd just been playing. The man looked it up, told Hallie what it was. Hallie thanked him and hung up the phone.

"Well, we have a cow who likes Beethoven," Hallie said to Myles and David. "Beethoven's Sixth Symphony to be exact. It's called the *Pastoral Symphony.*"

Myles nodded slowly. "Makes a kind of sense," he said.

"Why?" David asked.

"Pastoral means 'countrylike.' I suppose Cassie heard that in the music."

"Maybe that's what made her speak," said David. "Maybe she couldn't help herself when she heard it."

"Maybe," said Myles.

They sat silently, thinking about many things.

Finally David broke the silence. "Do you suppose

all cows can speak?" he asked his father.

"I don't even want to begin thinking about it," Myles said evenly.

David got up from the table and headed for the door. "Where are you going?" Myles asked.

"I'm going to tell a couple of people we have a talking cow," David said.

"I think we'd better wait awhile before we go telling anyone," said Myles quickly.

"How come?" David asked.

"It would just make me feel a bit easier," his father said. "I don't know if I'm ready for opening up a circus around here."

David nodded, sat down again, and kicked his feet slowly back and forth under his chair. "So what do we do now?" he said.

"About what?" Myles asked.

"We have a cow who talks," David said. "What do we do?"

"Well," said Myles. He took a deep breath and stared at the floor. "She wanted to hear Beethoven's Sixth Symphony, so I guess we go and find Beethoven's Sixth Symphony."

There wasn't a record store within ninety miles of Margaree Harbour. The closest one was in Sydney, so they called and asked if they had a recording of Beethoven's Sixth Symphony.

"Oh, we don't have records in the store," the salesman said with a laugh.

"Isn't this a record store?" Myles asked.

"Yes, it is," the salesman answered breezily.

"What do you handle then, if you don't handle records?" Myles asked.

"CDs and tapes," the salesman said. "No one has records anymore. In fact, I don't think they even make them."

Good news for Myles. He had three record players in his attic, and this made them valuable antiques. Myles thanked the man and hung up.

Now they had to figure out which they wanted, a tape or a CD.

"I have a Walkman," volunteered David.

"Me, too," said Hallie.

"If we can use a Walkman we won't have to buy her a whole new sound system."

They ran upstairs and came down with their

Walkmans. They strapped one of the small portables around Cassie's neck with a long cord, and tried to get the headphones to spread wide enough to fit over her big head, but it didn't work.

Myles then got his tool kit and they tried pulling the earpieces apart, soldering on additional sound wire and putting an earphone in each ear. But the earpieces were too small. They fell into Cassie's ear canals and drove her into a fit of sneezing.

"I guess we'd better try something else," Myles said, seeing more money flying out the window. Luckily they found a boom box at a garage sale that weekend, and it had a tape deck with automatic reverse. So they ordered a tape from Sydney, and Cassie was deliriously happy. For the time being.

CHAPTER V

C ASSIE WAS LYING DOWN, absorbed in her music. David sat on the ground next to her taking fistfuls of dirt and pouring them into a mound. The tape player was going full blast, and Beethoven's stirring, soaring music filled the air. Beethoven's Sixth Symphony was becoming quite familiar to David and he found himself sometimes humming along quietly. The more he heard it, the more he understood it, and the more he liked it. Which didn't happen very often. Usually when he heard a piece of music over and over he'd get bored with it. This music was different. The more he heard it, the better it got.

"Where does this come from?" Cassie asked.

"The music?" David asked.

Cassie nodded.

"Beethoven," said David.

"He wrote it all by himself?" Cassie asked incredulously.

"I'm pretty sure," said David.

Cassie shook her big head very slowly. It was too much for her to understand. "How does he know these things?" she asked, in awe. "How does he feel so much? And then once he feels these things, how does he make us feel along with him? How does he make sound tell us about open fields and green grass and hills and trees and streams and thunder and lightning? It's not as if he is imitating those sounds; thunder has a sound of its own, and so does a rushing stream, and his music reminds me of these things, but it doesn't exactly sound like them. Do you know what I mean?"

David nodded.

"I suppose you could imitate those things, if you were good enough, but lightning doesn't have a sound, nor do grass or trees; and yet I can *hear* them in his music. Can you hear them too, David?"

"Yes," said David.

"How does he do that?" Cassie asked.

David shook his head. "I don't know," he said.

Cassie moved her big head up and down slowly in time to the music. David watched his cow, amazed at how deeply affected she was by this one piece of music. Surely by now she knew the whole symphony by heart. She must have heard it over and over a hundred times without stopping.

"What makes the sound?" Cassie asked abruptly.

"Vibration," said David.

"Explain, please."

"Sound comes from things vibrating together," David explained, rubbing his hands together to give her the idea. "The vibration makes waves in the air and that makes our eardrums vibrate, and that's what makes music."

"What's vibrating in this case?" Cassie asked.

"Well, the speakers are vibrating," said David. He

held up the boom box for Cassie, showing her the speakers inside the protective case. Then he held it next to her face and let her feel the vibrations.

"And where is Beethoven and what is he doing to cause the vibrations?" Cassie asked.

"Beethoven's dead," said David.

Cassie went pale beneath her fur

"How did he die?" she asked, looking very concerned.

"I don't know," said David, "but don't worry, it wasn't recently. It must have happened about two hundred years ago."

"Then how can he be causing the vibrations?" Cassie asked.

"He wrote down the music when he was still living. Then he died," said David. "But other people, who are alive now, are playing it."

"What do you mean other people are playing it?" demanded Cassie.

"Musicians play the music."

"What are musicians?"

"They're people who play musical instruments, and they read the music Beethoven wrote, and that's how you can hear it."

"So somewhere a person is doing something that vibrates and that's how we can hear the Beethoven?" said Cassie, concentrating on this new information with all her might.

"Yes," said David, "except that it's probably about a hundred people doing the vibrating for this piece of music."

"Where are these people?" Cassie asked. She was beginning to look very agitated. "Why can't I see them?"

"I don't know where they are," David said. "They probably made this record a long time ago, and they're doing other things by now."

"I would like to see some of these things that vibrate," said Cassie. "Can you show me some?"

"Sure," said David, getting up. "I'll be right back."

David went in the house, rummaged through his father's bedroom, and came back with an old ukulele with a string missing.

"This is a musical instrument," said David. "It's what musicians play. This is what makes the vibrations you hear on the record."

"Do it," Cassie said.

"Play?" said David.

"Yes," Cassie said urgently.

"I don't know how."

"Do it anyway."

"It won't sound very good," said David.

He picked up the ukulele and tried strumming the way he saw his father do it. Some interesting noises came out of it, but not much that sounded like music.

"Anyway, that's an instrument," he said, putting down the ukulele, "and the strings are vibrating, and so is the air inside the hole. A lot of things are vibrating."

Cassie sniffed at the ukulele. "If I learned how to play this thing, could I play the music of Beethoven?" she asked.

"I don't think Beethoven has any ukuleles in his music," said David.

"What does he have in his music?" Cassie asked.

"Oh," said David, trying to think of some instruments that he might have heard in Beethoven's Sixth Symphony. "There's violins and drums and trumpets and flutes and piccolos and about a million other things."

"I want to see someone playing an instrument," said Cassie, with a new sense of urgency in her voice. "How do I do that? How do I see someone playing an instrument?"

"I'll be right back," said David and he went into the house again. In a few minutes he came back with a magazine. It was opened to a picture of a local boy playing an accordion. His hair was plastered back and shining and he had a huge smile on his face.

"Not a picture," said Cassie impatiently. "I want to see a real instrument. Played by a real person."

David thought about it for a minute. "I'll see what I can do," he said and he ran off down the road.

When he came back there was a girl with him. She was tall and thin with eyeglasses that slid down her nose. She wore a kilted skirt and a plaid hat and she carried a huge set of bagpipes. Her name was Natalie, and every afternoon she played the bagpipes in front of McCloud's. McCloud's was a store in the Harbour that sold Scottish goods to tourists. If the sun was shining she had a large umbrella to shade her; when it rained she wore a slicker.

"Okay," said Natalie suspiciously, when they got to Cassie's pen. "We're here. What's up?"

"I would just like to hear you play for a few minutes."

"I was just playing at McCloud's," said Natalie. "Why couldn't you hear me over there?"

David wasn't good at lying. He'd never had much reason to do it, and it made him uncomfortable, so he looked for a way of telling the truth without saying anything. "I want my cow to hear some music."

"What on earth for?" Natalie asked.

"I just think she would like it."

"You're crazy," said Natalie.

"No," said David. "She hasn't seemed happy recently and I think some music would be the thing."

"You want me to cheer up your cow?" Natalie asked, wrinkling her nose in disgust, which caused her eyeglasses to slip further down her nose.

"Just for a minute."

Natalie looked hard at David. She squinted her eyes, tightened one side of her mouth and put one hand on her hip. "If you tell anyone I did this, I'll kill you," she said.

"I won't," said David.

Natalie looked at him one last time to see if he was pulling some joke on her. She saw nothing but innocence looking back at her, so she put the large sack under her arm and began to blow. The bag filled up, her cheeks puffed out, and soon the wonderfully stirring whine of the bagpipes filled the air.

Cassie lifted her head, gasped, and her jaw dropped open.

David froze in fear, thinking Cassie might say something, but she restrained herself. He sat down next to Cassie and they listened as Natalie played.

David had heard Natalie every day for a year, on his way back from school, but today, through Cassie's ears, he heard her for the first time. Natalie was playing a Scottish dance tune that seemed very simple on the surface but if you listened carefully it had twists and turns and intricacies that were almost impossible to follow. The sound of the bagpipes was piercing and strident, but stirring at the same time. It was a whine and a wheeze but it made you want to stand up. To dance. To march. To hold yourself very proudly.

The tune finished abruptly and Natalie went right back to her pose with one hand on her hip, squinty eyes, and one corner of her mouth pursed. "Well?" she said.

"That was very good," said David.

"Is your cow happy now?"

"Yes," said David. "She's fine now."

Natalie gave him one last suspicious look, turned,

and went back to McCloud's Imported Scottish Goods Store. "'Bye," she said over her shoulder.

"That was the most amazing thing I've ever heard," said Cassie, when Natalie was out of earshot.

She stood up and shook herself ecstatically.

"My Lord, what an emotional experience! And she wasn't even playing Beethoven! What kind of music was that?"

"Scottish music," said David.

"When she started it sounded like someone was killing a pig. It was terrifying. But then you get used to the sound and the terror turns into something stirring and grand. How did that happen? How did she do that?"

"I don't know," said David.

"Magical," said Cassie. "What do they call those things she was playing?"

"Bagpipes," said David.

"Do they play those things in Beethoven?"

"I don't think so," said David.

"Why not?" asked Cassie.

"I don't think they use them in orchestras," David said.

"It would be a grand thing if they did," said Cassie.

CHAPTER VI

C ASSIE WAS GONE. Her gate was open and there was no sign of her anywhere.

"Where in the world could she be?" Hallie said.

"I don't know," said Myles. "Go down the road and knock on some doors and ask if anyone's seen her. David, you call Angus down at the police station, and I'll take the truck and look around up at the Forks."

Hallie ran down the road, David got on the phone,

and Myles jumped into his pickup truck and drove off. When he got to the gas station at the Forks he ran into Stuart McAllister, who was putting new windshield wipers on his truck.

"Say, don't you people have a brown-and-white cow?" Stuart called out.

"Yes, we do," said Myles.

"I just saw one running down route nineteen toward Nyanza."

"Thanks for the tip," said Myles and he ran back to his truck.

"You want to be closing the gate after her," McAllister shouted after him. "That's a good way to lose a cow!"

"I know all about it," Myles called out, and zoomed off down route nineteen.

Six miles out of town he spotted her, head down, puffing and fuming and barreling down the road at a good clip.

Myles pulled up along next to her and leaned out the window. "Where are you going?" he called in alarm.

"Sydney," said Cassie, moving along.

"What for?" Myles shouted again.

"There's a concert at the college auditorium. They're playing Beethoven!"

"It's ninety miles away!"

"I can make it," Cassie puffed, looking tired already.

"Cassie," Myles pleaded, "you just can't go wandering all over the countryside. Someone will take you away."

"I'll stay on the back roads."

"No, you can't do it, Cassie, it's dangerous."

Cassie stopped short and turned on Myles. "I am going to hear Beethoven!" she said. Her eyes were wide and her nostrils flared. She meant business.

A farmer nearby was fixing the blade on his plow. He looked up at all the commotion.

"Who you talkin' to?" he shouted.

"I'm talking to my cow," Myles called back.

"Who was it that answered?" the farmer said.

"Nobody," said Myles sharply.

"I heard you speak, then I heard someone else answer."

"It was me that answered," said Myles.

"It sounded like the cow," said the farmer.

"It was me," said Myles.

"Well, I'm glad to hear it," said the farmer. "I thought it was the cow. It made me a little anxious. If one of us is going crazy, I'd just as soon it was you!"

"It was just me," said Myles, and he tried to laugh a little laugh.

"I thought it was time for Martha to take me to the home!"

"No, you're okay," Myles said. "It was just me talking to myself."

The farmer smiled and waved and went back to what he was doing.

"Now look what you did," Myles said to Cassie. "The farmer thinks I'm going crazy."

"I don't care," said Cassie. "I'm going to hear Beethoven."

Myles drummed on the dashboard of his pickup. He bit his mustache. "Wait here for a minute," he said and got out of the pickup.

"Why?" Cassie asked suspiciously.

"You'll hear your Beethoven, but I've got to call David and Hallie. They're running all over town looking for you, worried half to death."

"I'll miss the concert."

"You won't miss the concert. I just have to pick them up and then we'll drive you there." Myles turned to the farmer. "Have you got a phone?" he called.

"No," said the farmer, "but they have one over at the Co-op."

Myles told Cassie to stay where she was. "I'll be right back," he said and he raced to the Co-op at the Forks and called home.

The line was busy. David was calling everyone on the island. On the third try he got through. He told David that he'd found Cassie, to look for Hallie, and to bring her back to the house.

"Why?" David asked.

"We're taking Cassie to Sydney," Myles said, and he hung up.

He raced back to Cassie and hid her in some trees.

"Don't you dare move," he threatened, and drove back to the harbor to pick up David and Hallie.

When they got back to where Miles had left Cassie, she was gone. Myles slammed on the brakes and jumped out of the truck. He took off his hat, pulled on his mustache, and looked around in every direction. No sign of her.

The old farmer was still fixing the blade on his plow. "Did you see any sign of my cow?" Myles called out.

"Yes," the farmer answered.

"Where'd she go?" Myles pressed.

"After you left I saw her sneaking out from behind those trees over there. She paced around for a while and then headed east. As she passed me she said, 'I can't wait around all day.'"

"Oh, I doubt that!" Myles said breezily.

"Yes, she did," said the farmer. "She said it clear as a bell."

Myles laughed a very stiff laugh. "Maybe your wife is right after all," he said.

"I don't think so," the farmer said suspiciously. "I heard her clear as day. You've got yourself a talking cow. I think you know it, too."

"Wouldn't that be something?" Myles called out and sped away.

In the rearview mirror he could see the farmer

watching them suspiciously as they drove into the distance.

"She's gone crazy," said Myles, speeding east. "She was a sweet and contented cow yesterday. What's happened to her?"

"Beethoven," said David softly, looking out the window. "Beethoven happened to her."

Five miles down the road they caught up with Cassie. She was moving at a furious pace, foaming at the mouth and sweating like a horse.

Myles pulled up alongside her and rolled down the window, but Cassie paid no attention. Myles beeped the horn.

"Hi there, remember me?" he said, waving.

"I haven't got time for small talk," Cassie said curtly, without looking over.

"We're going to take you to hear your Beethoven," Hallie called out the window, leaning over her father. "You'll never make it walking."

Cassie paid no attention.

"If this is what classical music does to you, I'm glad I'm ignorant of it," Myles said.

"It doesn't have this effect on everyone," said David.

"Just cows," said Myles, trying to hold on to his good humor.

He leaned out the window again. "Cassie, you've got to get into the truck. It's the only way you'll be safe. The police don't take kindly to stray cows, they'll stop you and tie you up and put you in a small pen. And if the police don't find you, there are some sly folks around that might think you're looking for a new home, if you know what I mean."

Cassie stopped and looked at Myles, not pleased with the news.

Myles pulled over, got out of the pickup, and walked over to her. "It's about forty-three more miles, Cassie," he said, patting her gently on her flank, "and the concert hall is in the middle of the city. They don't let cows wander around in cities."

"You win," said Cassie, her breath coming out in a rasp. "I'm bushed anyway. Just don't let me miss the Beethoven."

Myles opened the gate of the pickup and Cassie tried to climb in, but the truck bed was too high. She got her front legs up, but even with the three of them pushing and pulling, they couldn't get her back legs to go high enough.

"What now?" Hallie asked.

"We've got to get some boards so she can walk up into the truck," said Myles.

"I'll find a farm and borrow some planks. You two stay here. Just make sure she doesn't go wandering off again."

Myles drove off and soon came back with two planks. He opened the back gate, put them on the ground and leaned the other ends up into the truck. "Up and at 'em," he said with a wave.

Cassie gingerly stepped on the boards and wobbled up into the flatbed. The springs creaked and groaned and the tires looked dangerously flat, but miraculously the truck held her weight.

"Will we make it?" David asked.

"I hope so," said Myles, without much conviction. "You'd better lie down," he called out to Cassie. "I don't think this is legal."

Cassie did as she was told.

"She's still up too high," said Miles. "No one drives around with a cow in a pickup."

"How do we get her lower down in the truck?" Hallie asked.

Myles puffed out his cheeks and chewed on his mustache. "First we take back the boards, then we find a hardware store. We buy a tarpaulin and we cover her up. Maybe that will keep us out of trouble for a while."

He blew out a long breath and squeezed his eyes together with his fingers. "Why I'm going through with this, I do not know. All I wanted was a little bit of ice cream."

They drove to the farm, returned the planks, then headed for the nearest hardware store and bought a plastic orange tarpaulin. They tied the tarpaulin down over Cassie and went on to Sydney, praying that the truck wouldn't get a flat or break a shock.

CHAPTER VII

S YDNEY IS NOT A BIG CITY as cities go, but
 to Hallie and David it was enormous. Margaree
Harbour, where they had spent their whole lives, con-
sisted of nothing but a general store, McCloud's
Imports, and a gas station, so a trip to Sydney was
always an adventure. As for Cassie, under ordinary cir-
cumstances she would have found the trip to Sydney
exhilarating, but this occasion she was oblivious to

everything. Her mind was only on Beethoven.

Once they arrived in Sydney Myles drove by the concert hall, found a quiet side street, parked, and went to get pizza for dinner. He left Hallie and David at the truck to try and keep Cassie under control. She moved her big head under the tarp to get the stiffness out of her neck just as an elderly couple passed by.

"Wowee!" said the man, jumping a foot in the air. "What you got under the tarp?"

"Just a few chickens!" Hallie called out breezily.

"Those are some pretty hefty chickens!" the man said, laughing.

"Keep still," David growled to Cassie when the couple got out of earshot. "Don't move around so much."

"I'm doing the best I can," Cassie whispered from under the tarp.

Myles came back with two big pizzas and a bag of salad. He shoved the salad under the tarp for Cassie, and the three of them ate their pizzas in the cab of the truck. When they finished they drove back to the college. Myles stopped the car across the street from the hall. "Wait here," he said, getting out of the truck. "I'll walk around the building and see if there's a quiet place we can park and still hear the music."

"Someplace where we can *hear* the music?" said Cassie in alarm, from under the tarp. "That's no good. I have to *see* this concert. I have to see the musicians playing."

"Why?" Myles asked, setting his baseball hat low on his forehead, his patience just this short of snapping. "Why do you have to see them playing?"

"I *have* to," said Cassie with finality. "I didn't come all this way to do what I can do at home. I want to see living musicians."

"Cows can't go into concert halls," said Hallie.

"Why is that?" Cassie asked, shocked at the news.

"There's no seating arrangement for cows," said Hallie.

"I'll stand in the back," said Cassie.

"It isn't done," said Myles, getting more than a little aggravated. "Cows don't go to concerts. That is a firm rule. There's no arbitrating. I'll have to put my foot down on that one."

"Is there a law?" Cassie asked.

"Probably."

"But you're not sure?"

"I've never seen a cow in a concert hall, so there must be a law," said Myles, not mentioning that he'd never been to a concert himself.

"I'm going to see the concert!" Cassie said through clenched teeth. "One way or another I'm going to see them play Beethoven. I wanted this to be a simple thing. That's why I left without telling you. I *knew* you would make complications and give me arguments."

"Cassie, without us you'd still be fifty miles away," Hallie pleaded, looking for a hint of reasonable behavior. "You wouldn't be here at all."

"I am going to see this concert!" Cassie growled. She tossed the tarpaulin off with a shrug of her head, threw one leg over the side of the truck, and started out.

"Get back in!" said Myles angrily, throwing the tarp back over her and pushing her down. "Just get back in. We'll figure out something. Just don't make a disturbance." Myles leaned against the truck and wiped his face with a red checkered handkerchief. Cassie tried to settle herself down under the tarp, but she was huffing and puffing from all the emotion.

"Wait here, I'll be right back," said Myles.

"Where are you going?" David asked uneasily.

"I'm going to look for another way into the hall," Myles said, walking off. A minute later he appeared around the other side of the building.

"There's a big double door around back," he said walking over to the truck. "It goes into the basement and no one's around." He pointed to Hallie. "You and David try her out and see if you can find your way to the stage. Maybe there's a place we can get to without anyone noticing."

"What if we get caught?" David asked.

"Just say you're looking for the bathroom."

"Isn't this illegal?" Hallie asked.

"Probably," said Myles.

"We're not dressed too well for a concert," Hallie said, looking down at her dirty jeans and sneakers and sweatshirt.

"Can't be helped," Myles said.

Hallie took a deep breath. "Okay," she said, "here goes nothing." She grabbed David by the hand and the two of them ran off.

They quickly found the double doors in the back of

the building, opened them quietly, and saw in front of them a dark hallway filled with pieces of stage sets, pianos, kettle drums, harps, and all sorts of props. Doors led everywhere. Trying to look casual, they soon found a stairway that led to big black doors. It had STAGE written on it in big letters. They opened it cautiously. Behind the doors were huge black curtains enveloping the back and sides of the stage. "Maybe we can twist Cassie up in one of these things," David whispered, flapping one of the black velvet curtains as gently as he was able. He and Hallie twisted the huge drape around them, testing it out, and after a minute they felt safe and well hidden. There seemed to be enough room inside the curtains to hide all of them. They peered out, saw no one, and started back outside.

Halfway back, they took a wrong turn and stumbled into a huge dressing room. Dozens of musicians were practicing scales, putting strings on violins, oiling trumpet valves, and standing around half dressed. "Hi!" one of them called out warmly, as he saw David and Hallie. He was in a white tie and tails and polka-dot undershorts and carried a French horn under his arm. Hallie and David waved and backed out of the room.

No one seemed to care about their being there. "That was a close one," David said when they were well out of the upper hallway. When they saw the exit, they breathed a sigh of relief and ran outside.

"How'd you make out?" Myles asked, when he saw them coming around the building.

"We found a way to the stage," said Hallie. "No guards. Nothing. The whole place was completely empty except for fifty musicians in their underwear. What do we do now?"

"We just have to wait till it gets dark and try to smuggle Cassie in," said Myles skeptically, chewing on his mustache. "Unless someone has a better idea."

"Not me," said Hallie.

"Me, neither," David echoed.

"Why are we doing this?" Myles asked no one in particular. He shook his head, closed his eyes and leaned back in his seat.

For the next hour they stayed by the truck, watching the darkness settle in. At about seven-thirty the audience began to arrive in dribs and drabs, laughing and joking in anticipation of the evening. By eight o'clock, the auditorium was almost full. At 8:05 the streets emptied and the ushers closed the doors. Myles took a deep breath. "It's now or never," he said. He started the truck's motor and slowly drove to the back of the building, keeping the lights off. When he got to the rear doors he shut off the engine, got out of the cab, looked around cautiously, and dropped the back gate of the pickup.

"Uh-oh," said Myles, chewing on his mustache.

"What's the matter?" Hallie asked.

"No boards," said Myles. "We can't get Cassie out of the truck."

"Don't worry, don't worry," said Cassie impatiently, waving everyone aside. "Just get out of the way."

"What for?" said David.

"Just move away!" says Cassie.

Everyone backed up at her command, and Cassie made a flying leap out of the truck. "Whuumph!" she said and she skidded to a thunderous stop with her forelegs crumpling beneath her, and her chin smashing into the ground.

"Ye Gods," Hallie said, rushing over to help her up. "Are you all right?

"I'm fine, I'm fine," Cassie said, waving her away.

"You've hurt yourself," said Hallie.

"I'm fine," said Cassie, pushing her away. "Let's go!" She staggered to her feet and started to walk shakily toward the back doors, limping badly.

Myles opened the doors, and just at that moment an awesome sound came pouring out of the building. Cassie gasped and stopped in her tracks. "What in heaven's name is that?" she asked, the hair standing up on the back of her neck.

"They're tuning up," said Hallie. "Come on, let's go," she said, and she tried to push Cassie into the building. But Cassie didn't budge. She stood transfixed, listening to one of the world's strangest and most magical sounds. The sound of an entire orchestra tuning up their instruments. It is the moment in time when everyone in the orchestra stops being separate people and slowly turns into one thing. One idea. One person. One instrument. Without saying it, or even knowing it, the orchestra is saying to the audience, "Something extraordinary is about to happen!" There is the promise of exquisite joy and happiness just around the corner. Like Christmas morning and your first look at the presents under the tree. Like the moment before the guests arrive for your birthday party, or the first day of summer. All of these things the orchestra is telling you, and then it says, "Once you get past this moment, this magical, almost frightening moment where nothing has quite happened yet, this moment where anything is possible, your life just may possibly change forever."

"Oh, my," Cassie said, coming back to life. "Oh, my."

"Come on!" rasped Hallie, not understanding what was holding things up. Cassie pulled herself together and hurried on, quietly following the sound. Finding their way again they tiptoed back to the stage, and just as they got to the doors, a man passed in front of them. He was carrying a ladder. They froze in terror. The man looked at the four of them, nodded and kept going. Hallie and David looked at each other in amazement. What could he have been thinking? It was as if seeing a cow backstage was an everyday occurrence. When he had gone, they opened the stage doors and made a passage for Cassie between the curtains and the wall. Hallie and David led the way with Cassie in the middle and Myles behind, holding down the curtain so it didn't bulge too much. Just as they settled themselves, carefully gathering the curtain around them, the audience began to applaud.

"What's going on? What's happening?" Cassie asked urgently, struggling to see.

"The conductor just came out," said David, peeking through a small hole in the curtain. He found another hole for Cassie and draped the curtain around one of her horns so that the hole stayed in front of an eye. "Thanks," she mumbled, preoccupied with the wonderful sight in front of her.

The conductor bowed to the audience. Then he turned toward the orchestra, raised his baton, and stood motionless as a statue for what seemed like an hour, lost in the deepest silence Cassie had ever heard. Not a sound in the audience; not a sound from the musicians; not a sound anywhere. Then all of a sudden the conductor leaped into the air, landed hard on his platform and threw his arms down wildly. All in one motion. And the trumpets went crazy.

"Wow!" shrieked Cassie in delight.

"Shhhh! I said," said Hallie, "and I mean it! One more sound and we're leaving!"

"Sorry," said Cassie automatically, lost in the excitement of the music and the people playing, seeing for the first time the instruments—the beautiful pieces of polished wood and shining metal—and those sounds! What sounds! Before now, the only music she knew had come out of a small cassette player on top of her stall. It hadn't prepared her for the power and range and subtlety of what came through those wonderful music machines. Hearing the music this close vibrated her whole body. It came through the air with a wallop, hitting her as a real physical force, caressing and washing and massaging her. And those sounds! The ringing of the brass! The buzz of the bows on the strings! The shock and danger of the drums, the piercing purity of the flutes and oboes . . . the pompousness of the bassoons! It was almost too exciting. And the *seriousness* of the musicians! Such energy pouring out of them! And the looks on their faces! As if their lives depended on each note.

David found a program on the floor and picked it up "'*Rodeo*,'" he read, "'by Aaron Copeland. A suite for orchestra based on his ballet of the same name.'"

They stood and listened in awe to this exciting, sweeping, simple piece that somehow made them think of deserts and prairies and cowboys and sunsets, and when it was over it was all they could do to keep from shouting *Bravo!* and applauding wildly along with the audience. The conductor bowed, and they immediately began the next piece, which was a symphony by Mozart. The symphony was light and airy and comfortable and very different from the Beethoven they'd all gotten to know so well. This Mozart person (if you could tell from his music) seemed gentler and calmer than Beethoven. "Everything's okay! Everything's in order," his music seemed to say. And even Myles and Hallie started having a good time.

"Classical music isn't so bad once you get used to it," Hallie whispered to her father. Myles had to agree.

After the Mozart there was an intermission. They audience got up and stretched and coughed and talked among themselves. They discussed the performance and read their programs. A flute player, practicing a difficult passage, came wandering into the wings and banged right into Cassie. "Whoops," he said to her as he bounced back. "Pardon me." Hallie and David looked at each other in horror, but again nothing happened.

After a few minutes, the audience wandered back into the hall and took their seats. The conductor came out and again was greeted by a great applause. He bowed, turned to the orchestra, raised his arms, and did the same leap, abruptly throwing his arms down and then up, which seemed to start the orchestra. *PA PA PA PAAAAAH!!! PA PA PA PAAAAAH!!* the music went, strong and stirring and courageous.

"What are they doing?" Cassie said with alarm. "That's not Beethoven."

"Yes, it is," said David.

"No, it's not," said Cassie. "I know Beethoven by heart, that's not him!"

"You only know his Sixth Symphony," said David. "This is his Fifth."

"Oh, my goodness!" said Cassie. "How many did he write?"

"About nine or ten. And a lot of other things, too."

"Like what?"

"Piano concertos and violin concertos and chamber music; all kinds of things," said David.

"How did you know that?" Hallie asked.

"Vivian told me," David said, predictably.

As Beethoven's Fifth Symphony continued, Cassie listened to it, transfixed. The power of the music beat into Cassie's heart and soul, her eyes glazed over, her mouth hung open, and she began drooling on the floor.

"Stop that!" David said sharply, when he noticed.

"Sorry," said Cassie, blinking rapidly and snapping her mouth shut. David wiped up her drool with a paper napkin saved from the pizza.

For the rest of the concert Cassie was silent. She was silent when the symphony was over. She was silent when the audience stood on their feet cheering wildly. So were Hallie, David, and Myles. They knew that they had heard something important. Something that spoke of places inside them that they needed to go to. Places that everyone needed to go. They stayed silent as they left the hall and gathered themselves together in the truck.

On the way home, when they were in the country-side again, Cassie leaned her big head into the cab. The wind was blowing sixty miles an hour, and she shouted over the noise. "My goodness!" she said. "Wasn't *that* something, now! Beethoven's Fifth Symphony! Not too shabby! It's got the same wonderful energy and power as the Sixth, but in *this* symphony he's not making pictures with the music. It's about feelings. It's as if he's trying to tear his insides open and shake himself loose. And shake the world loose, too. It makes me want to grab a flag and run to all the cows of the world and liberate them. 'Be free!' I want to shout at them, 'Free yourselves! Throw away your chains! Pull out the nose rings and the bells around your necks! Stamp flat your milk pails and be free!' My goodness! The courage in that music! It makes you want to face everything bravely with your chin up and your chest out. It makes you feel that you'll never be afraid of anything ever, ever again."

As they drove home, they all began to talk about the music, trying to sing snatches of it. "PA PA PA PAAAAAH! PA PA PA PAAAAH!" Cassie mooed at the top of her voice, freeing the trees and the nesting birds and the insects and the frogs and the cows in the fields.

CHAPTER VIII

T HE NEXT DAY WAS SATURDAY. The family was having breakfast when Cassie's big head came pushing through the kitchen window.

"Good morning," Myles said with a mouthful of oatmeal.

"I have to learn how to play an instrument," Cassie said, too excited to greet anyone.

"What brought that on?" said Hallie.

"I have to play the music of Beethoven. It's the only way I'll ever know what it's like to feel like him."

"Why do you have to feel like Beethoven?" asked Myles.

"I have to feel that big, that courageous, that strong, that free."

"I'm not sure that will do it," said Myles.

"I'm quite sure it will," said Cassie.

"What instrument do you want to learn?" David asked.

"Well, my preference would be the flute," said Cassie.

"I don't think that would work out," Hallie said, actually thinking about it for a moment.

"It's a very beautiful instrument," said Cassie. "Very shiny and small and you can hear it clearly no matter what else is happening."

"I don't think it's for you," said Hallie.

"Why not?" asked Cassie.

"You need ten fingers. I don't know much about music, but I know you need all your fingers for the flute."

"I'm sure something could be worked out," said Cassie.

"It's a long shot," said Myles.

"Then how about the trumpet?" Cassie asked.

"It's also a very small instrument," said Myles. "It would be the same problem as the flute. It's got three small valves and you have to press them down. That needs fingers. You couldn't get your hoof around them. You would also need another hand to hold it up."

"Can we at least look into it?" Cassie asked, slightly put out by Myles's lack of enthusiasm.

"Well, let's see about that," said Myles.

"No, I'll check into it," Hallie said, and she wrote herself a note.

Myles cleared his throat. "Cassie, could you excuse us for a minute?"

"Certainly," said Cassie. Myles waited for her to leave but nothing happened. "Just go back outside for a while, would you?" he said as pleasantly as he could.

"Why?" Cassie asked.

"Just go back outside. We have to have a talk. Just the three of us."

"Oh! Well, pardon me!" Cassie said with more than a hint of sarcasm in her voice, and she backed away from the window. Myles quickly got up and closed it behind her.

"We can't have this," Myles said soberly.

"Can't have what?" said David.

"We can't spend our days and nights following the dictates of a cow. She's taking up too much time."

"No, she isn't," David protested.

"Yes, she is," Myles insisted. "We can't spend our lives looking for musical instruments for a cow. Now you both have work to do, and it's not getting done."

"It is getting done," said Hallie. "We're doing everything we're supposed to do."

"But it takes you till midnight to do it. And your homework isn't getting finished, and you're both exhausted. You know the deal. We said from the beginning that she was your responsibility. If you can't handle her . . ."

"You're not getting rid of my cow!" said David fiercely.

"I'm not talking about getting rid of her," said Myles. "I'm talking about treating her like a cow. Not a human being."

"She is a human being," says David. "She has rights."

"She's not a human being," said Myles. "She's a cow."

"Well, she's a mammal," David protested, "and she can talk. And she's more interesting than most people I know, anyway. And besides, we're learning important things because of her. She's taking us on an adventure."

"We don't need adventures. We need milk," said Myles.

"She's giving us milk," said David.

"Plus," said Hallie, "we're sitting on a gold mine."

"Enough said," Myles said. He stood up and wiped his mouth. "You both know what I'm talking about. And I'm done with her. I have a life to lead. She's your responsibility."

"Didn't you have a good time yesterday?" David demanded. "Didn't you like the music?"

"Yes, I did," Myles confessed. "I enjoyed it. If it wasn't for the three heart attacks she gave me, I'd say I had a very good day. But now I have bills to pay, and a business to run, and two children to take care of who both have bags under their eyes."

"Does that mean we can't find her an instrument?" Hallie asked.

"It means that you have to do your work and get

your sleep, and I'm not baby-sitting a cow anymore."

Myles left the house, went out to his workroom and began banging on things. Hallie opened the kitchen window and called Cassie. "We'll see what we can do," she said quietly, "but we can't promise anything."

"Oh, thank you, thank you!" Cassie said, almost crying in gratitude.

"How do we get a trumpet for Cassie to try?" David asked later, on their way to school. "Is there someone in Margaree who plays?"

"Not that I know of," Hallie said, "except in the school band."

"Maybe we can borrow one from Mr. Katzenbach," said David, "just for a day or so."

"You can't just borrow instruments," said Hallie. "We'd have to tell him something."

"Like what?" David asked.

"Like we're thinking of joining the orchestra and don't know which instrument we want to play. Something like that."

"That might work," said David.

Hans Katzenbach was the music teacher for the

whole school. There were never enough people for the orchestra, so when Hallie and David told him of their interest in joining he was delighted. He unlocked the instrument room and came back with a trumpet. It was pretty banged up and the valves were sticky, but it played, as he demonstrated by doing a section from "Flight of the Bumble Bee," which he performed brilliantly. He handed the trumpet to Hallie. "Keep it for a couple of days," he said. "See how you like it." They thanked him and took it home.

"Look what we have, Cassie!" David shouted happily, running down the driveway and holding up the gleaming trumpet for Cassie to see. "Oh, my!" said Cassie with wonder in her eyes. She sat down on her haunches and looked at it reverently. Then cautiously she tried to pick it up but her hoofs couldn't find anything to grab. The trumpet kept falling in the dirt. Each time she dropped it David picked it up, cleaned it off, and handed it back. "Hmmm," Cassie said disapprovingly, after her fourth attempt to hang on to it. "They could have made it less slippery and put those plungers further apart."

"They made it for people, not cows," said Hallie.

"Here," said David. "I'll hold it and you try to blow." He held the trumpet up to Cassie's face. "Blow," he ordered, once he found what seemed to be the center of her lips. Cassie tried to blow into the mouthpiece, but the trumpet kept sliding into her mouth and banging against her teeth. "Don't push so hard," she said harshly to David.

"I have to push to make the pressure," David said. "That's what gets the sound." He concentrated on getting the mouthpiece in the exact center of her mouth, and Cassie tried again to purse her lips, but her mouth wouldn't go into the right shape. When she blew into the mouthpiece nothing but wind came out.

"Do it harder," said David. "Blow harder." Cassie blew harder, but the only sound that came out was the sound of the sea.

"I think it's broken," said Cassie out of the side of her mouth, trying to speak around the tiny mouthpiece. "This isn't my instrument." She huffed, and turned away from the horn.

"You didn't give it enough time," said David. "You can't learn how to play a trumpet in five minutes."

"It's not my instrument!" said Cassie impatiently. "I

need something with more body. Something I can wrap myself around."

"Like what?" David asked.

"Like maybe that big violin."

"Which big violin?"

"The one that goes between the legs."

"That's called a cello."

"That's the one. I think the cello is my instrument."

David and Hallie went back to Mr. Katzenbach.

"The trumpet isn't for us," they said.

"Why not?" Mr. Katzenbach asked.

"Too loud," said Hallie. "We have neighbors who are old and sick."

Mr. Katzenbach shook his head mournfully and took the trumpet back into the instrument room.

"I was thinking maybe the cello might be a good idea," David called out to him.

"That's all the way in another direction," said Mr. Katzenbach. "If you want one thing then you won't want the other."

"Well," said Hallie, "I think we don't want the one thing. I think what we want is the other."

"All right," said Mr. Katzenbach, shrugging his

shoulders, "give it a try." He went rummaging noisily in the instrument room and came back with a cello. He sat down with it and played some Bach for a few minutes, just to see if it was in working order. Then, satisfied that it was in playing shape, he put it in a cloth case and handed it to Hallie.

"Thank you, Mr. Katzenbach," she said. "We'll take good care of it."

That afternoon they brought Cassie the cello. Her eyes lit up. "Yes," she cooed, "this is more like it." David took the cello out of the case and held it up for Cassie to see. Cassie walked around the instrument, examining it from all sides.

"It's more cumbersome than I remembered," she said.

"You're supposed to play it sitting on a chair," said David.

"Well, that's out," said Cassie.

"If you sit on the ground and lean back against something it might work," said David.

"Maybe," Cassie said. "Let's give it a try." She sat down in the grass and put her back up against the wall of her pen.

"You have to go farther back," said David. "You have

to get your legs up in the air. You'll have to play the notes with your left hoof and pull on the bow with your right."

"One thing at a time," said Cassie, slowly settling back on her haunches and trying to lift her front feet off the ground. "I can't get these things up high enough," she said, straining her muscles to do things they weren't designed to do. "Push the cello in underneath me," she groaned. "I'll climb up with my front legs and use it for support."

"You'll scratch it all up," David said.

"Well, we have to do something," Cassie said impatiently, her back ready to cave in.

"Maybe we have to dig a hole underneath you."

"What good will that do?"

"You'll be able to lean back in it like a chair. Then you can use your front legs."

"Good idea," said Cassie, already worried about the plan.

David dug a deep hole next to where Cassie was sitting. It took him the better part of the afternoon. "There," he said when it was finished. "Try that out."

Cassie eased her rear end into the hole and leaned back gingerly.

"How does that feel?" David asked.

"I'll get used to it," Cassie said uneasily.

"Can you raise yourself up?" David asked.

"I'll give it a try," Cassie said warily. She lifted her front legs off the ground and found that the back wall of the hole held her weight. "Hand me the instrument," she said. David picked up the cello and put it between her forelegs. It stayed pretty much in place. "So far so good," Cassie said. "Now what do we do?"

"Well, you're supposed to hold up the bow now, but . . ."

"I know, I know," Cassie interrupted, "get some adhesive tape, we'll stick it on."

David ran into the house and came back with some electrician's tape. He pulled off a long strip, and taped the bow to Cassie's right front leg. "What do I do now?" Cassie asked brusquely.

"Now you rub the bow back and forth across the strings," David said, trying to remember what he'd seen Mr. Katzenbach do at the concert. Cassie started rubbing the cello strings with the bow. Terrible sounds came out. Tortured cat sounds. Back fence, midnight loneliness sounds. Grumbling, whining, and

91

disgruntled sounds. "Not quite what I expected," said Cassie. "If I remember correctly, there was more melody in this thing."

"Try stuff with the left leg," David said.

"Like what?"

"Move your left leg over the strings. That's how you change the sound. That's how you get different notes."

Cassie tried to do it. She slid her foreleg back and forth over the strings but the cat fight just got more intense. Far away a dog began barking. For several hours Cassie struggled with the instrument, trying desperately to get some semblance of tune or melody from it, but the cello was being tortured and it let her know. David went into the house and did his homework. When he came out the cello was on the ground and Cassie was moping in her pen.

"They gave you a broken cello," she said over her shoulder.

David was kind enough not to contradict her. They sat for a while in silence. Suddenly Cassie turned. She took a deep breath and sat up as straight as she could. "Well," she said, "enough of that. Onward! That's what

Ludwig would have said, isn't it? TA TA TA DAAAAAH!! See what happens? I hum a little of the Fifth and I can go on! Onward! I will NOT accept defeat. I am the master of my fate. TA TA TA DAAAAAH! How about drums?" Cassie asked, undaunted.

"Same problem as the cello. You'd have to sit back in a hole and wave your arms around a lot. We'd have to tie the sticks to your hoofs. And anyway they don't use drums in Beethoven."

"They do," Cassie corrected. "I saw them. Big ones that look like giant soup bowls."

"Kettle drums," said David. "I think you'd get bored with them after a while. They're loud and showy but they only get played every ten minutes or so."

"This is what we'll do," said Cassie. "We'll make a list of all the instruments that play Beethoven. One of them's bound to be the right one. Find me pictures. We'll decide from there." She got up, turned abruptly from David and began munching furiously on some grass.

The next day David went to the library and came back with an encyclopedia of music. He and Cassie pored over pictures of the instruments, examining each one, trying to see if any one of them could fit around her big body. A body that had hoofs instead of hands and fingers. But each instrument had terrible short-comings. The violin and viola were too small, and the bass violin was so big that it needed to be played standing up, which was impossible for Cassie. The French horn was out, because for some reason you had to put one hand inside the thing, and the mouthpiece was even smaller than the trumpet's. The clarinet needed all ten fingers and you had to pull your lips into a strange smile, and of course Cassie couldn't do that. The oboe was even worse. It had two reeds to the clarinet's one, and you had to blow into it as hard as the bagpipes.

"This one has possibilities," said Cassie, looking at a picture of a bassoon.

"No, it's no good," said David. "It's dangerous."

"How so?" Cassie asked.

"I saw someone play the bassoon at last year's grad-uation show, and in the middle of something called 'The Thieving Magpie' his face turned purple and he passed out. They had to stop the concert and put a cold compress on his head."

So much for the bassoon. The harp you had to pluck (ten fingers again), and the piano, well, there was no point in even thinking about the piano. With each instrument, Cassie became more and more discouraged.

"Maybe the glockenspiel," David said hopefully, holding up the picture halfheartedly, but Cassie just walked away.

"This is starting to get ridiculous," said Hallie when David told her about their afternoon.

"Why?" David asked.

"You know as well as I do," said Hallie.

"She's a genius," said David. "She needs nurturing."

There's a joke they tell about the people of Cape Breton. "How do you throw a party on the Cape?" the joke goes, and the answer is: "You pull your car off the road and you open the hood." Everyone laughs, but it's true. If someone on the island has a problem, no matter what it is, everyone drops whatever they're doing and they deal with it. It doesn't matter what the problem is or whose it is. It could be a family member, a neighbor, a passerby, or someone you don't even like.

It could be a car that doesn't start, a roof that leaks, a boat that won't float, or a knife that won't open. A lot of it is curiosity, a lot is neighborliness, but more importantly it's about sticking together in a place where you need cooperation in order to survive. In spite of himself, Myles was hooked. He had to help Cassie. Not because he was interested in her quest, or even because he liked her that much. It was because he was a Cape Bretoner and he couldn't stop himself.

"I have an idea," he said later that evening, while looking at some pictures of the brass instruments. "I'm not positive it will work, but it's worth a try."

"What's your idea, Dad?" David asked.

"The tuba," said Myles. "It's a big fat instrument. I think Cassie could find the mouthpiece, and maybe we can rig it so she can get a hoof on those huge keys."

"It's worth a try," said David.

The next day he went back to Mr. Katzenbach. "I think it's the tuba," he said. Mr. Katzenbach was not a patient man, but he held his frustration inside.

"The tuba?" he asked suspiciously. David nodded. Mr. Katzenbach gave David a long searching look to see if some sort of joke was being played on him. He saw nothing but innocence staring back. Whatever David was doing, Mr. Katzenbach needed players in the band. He sighed, went rummaging in the instrument room again, and came out with a beat-up old tuba. He sat down with it and played a brilliant rendition of "The Minute Waltz," to make sure it worked, and gave it to David to take home for yet another tryout. That afternoon David brought the tuba to his father in the shop. Myles looked it over carefully and took some measurements. "Just leave it with me for a while," he said.

The next day he called to David as he was walking past the shop. "Take a look at this," he said. "Tell me what you think." He pulled a cloth off the thing he'd been working on. Behind it was a rig that looked like a small version of the Eiffel Tower. The tuba was cradled high in the middle of it, protected by a blanket. "It's pretty rigid," he said, pushing on the mouthpiece with the flat of his hand. "No matter how clumsy she gets with it, she won't knock it over. What do you think?"

"Good," David said, nodding in appreciation. They carried it to the shed and presented it to Cassie. She sniffed at it suspiciously.

"Give it a try, Cassie," David said.

Cassie got up and walked around the wooden tower. She pushed at the tuba with her nose, examined the mouthpiece, licked it a couple of times, and then very tentatively blew into it. A low groan came out of the other end. Cassie started and jumped back. "Hmmmm . . ." she said, somewhat hopefully. She tried it again, and again she got a sound out of it—something between a foghorn and a moo. "Interesting," she said. "Sort of familiar." She tried again, with the same result. "Well, it's a sound anyway," she said, a bit encouraged in spite of herself. "How do you work the plungers?"

"Sit back in the hole," said Myles. "We'll push the thing over to you and see what happens when you lift up your front legs." Cassie walked over to the hole and lowered herself into it. She wriggled her bottom around in the dirt till it felt secure, craned her neck forward to find the mouthpiece, and gave another short blast. Then she lifted her right leg to find one of the valves. She couldn't see them so David placed her hoof in the middle of them. The hoof covered all four valves, so hitting just one would be difficult.

"What do I do now?" Cassie asked.

"Blow into the mouthpiece, then push down on the valves with your hoof," said David. Cassie licked her lips and blew into the mouthpiece, banging her hoof up and down on the valves at the same time. Strange noises came out of the horn. Gurgling wind rustlings. Stomach growls. Many things that would have been interesting on a sound-effects record, but nothing much in the way of music. Cassie strained at the instrument, trying to make her hoof hit individual keys, but her hoof was too big even for the tuba. Even if it had been smaller there wasn't enough feeling in the hoof to tell her what key she was hitting, and keeping the position of her leg around the instrument was impossible. After an hour she pushed herself out of the hole, limped to her shed, and lay down facing the wall. Not a word. Myles and David took the tuba out of the tower and put it back in the case. Then they went back to see Cassie. David sat down in the dirt next to her.

"We don't know what else to do," he said.

"Thanks for trying," Cassie said mournfully.

"Maybe you should think about other things," David said, trying to be practical.

"There is no reason to live anymore."

"Well now, that's a little dramatic," said Myles. "There are other things in life."

"I must learn to play Beethoven," Cassie said.

"It's not going to work," Myles said. "You're not built to play a musical instrument. Beethoven didn't write for cows. If he knew you personally, I'm sure he would have, but he didn't and there we are."

"You don't understand," Cassie said mournfully. "I never asked to hear Beethoven. I never asked for music to come into my life. This was something you brought to me, and I thank you for it, but the gift, as beautiful as it was, changed me, and I can't go back. It's just not possible. I am hungry for music and this hunger is deeper in me and more important to me than food or water or even breathing. It gives meaning to everything I do. I'm afraid I can't live without Beethoven. My soul calls out to play his beautiful music. I have to merge with him, you see, but he is dead, so what am I to do? How else can I merge with him but to play?"

"How about listening? What's wrong with that?" Myles asked. Cassie didn't answer. When the gloom got too heavy to bear Myles and David went for a walk.

"Life is hard," said David.

"Naaah," Myles snorted, "she's just being a bit dramatic. She likes the attention."

"Don't you think she's suffering?" David asked.

"If she is she'll get over it," said Myles. "This won't kill her, you know."

They walked on in silence, then Myles stopped short, a concentrated look on his face.

"What is it?" David asked.

"I have an idea," Myles said. "Give me a little time to see if I can make it work."

CHAPTER IX

For THE NEXT FEW DAYS, nobody saw much of Myles. They heard him banging away in the workroom behind the shop, but he wouldn't let anyone in. Then the following afternoon, on the way back from school, Hallie and David saw him laying out something in the field behind the house.

"What're you doing?" Hallie called.

"Come take a look," Myles shouted back. He started

dragging some huge rolled-up thing to the far end of the field. It had a great jumble of wires hanging like spaghetti down from one side, and it was all connected to a couple of huge electrical-outlet plugs.

"What is it?" David asked.

"You'll see in a minute," said Myles. He pushed the wires to one side with his feet and began rolling out what looked like an enormous piece of cotton bandage. What it was, actually, was five Mylar drop cloths cut in half longways and sewed together to make a ribbon thirty feet long and two feet wide. Once it was rolled out you could see black rectangles all down the cloth in sets of two and three, separated by white stripes. At every mark, both black and white, a wire came out of the cloth. All the wires ran to a big box. A big amplifier, it looked like. Hallie and David ran over and examined it.

"Do you know what it is?" Myles said, a mysterious smile on his face.

"No," Hallie said.

"Cassie will know," said Myles. He called to her. "Cassie, come and take a look at this." Cassie turned her big head around from the shed, where she'd been moping in the dark for days. "Come on over," Myles said. "I think this will interest you."

"Why?" Cassie asked, without enthusiasm. For days she'd been busy making everyone feel guilty about her failure of a life. As if not being able to find an instrument was everyone else's fault.

"Come and see this for yourself," Myles said, standing by his invention, hands on his hips while Cassie made up her mind. Cassie sighed and lumbered to her feet. She shuffled painfully over to the contraption. "What's this?" she asked. Myles said nothing. Cassie nudged it with her nose. "What is it?" she asked again.

"Figure it out," Myles said quietly. He stood there, smiling and saying nothing. Cassie walked down the edge of the Mylar ribbon, sniffing it as she went. Tentatively she put a hoof on the ribbon and pawed it. *CLANK!* it went. Startled at the noise, Cassie jumped back and waited for something else to happen. Nothing did. She pawed it again. It clanked again. She looked at Myles, who smiled but still said nothing. Cassie touched the cloth in another place. *CLANK!* it went again, this time in a higher pitch. She touched it on a few more spots. On each one she heard a *CLANK!*

"It's a piano!" said David, eyes wide and his hand up to his face. "You made a gigantic piano!"

Slowly Cassie registered what David had said, then she walked down the length of the cloth. Every few feet she reached out and touched the edge with her hoof. Each time she touched it there was a different sound. She started breathing heavily. "I want to walk on it," she said to Myles, trying to hold back her excitement.

"Go ahead," Myles said.

Cassie got on the cloth and tiptoed all the way down one way and then the other. At each rectangle there was a different sound. "I'm playing a scale, I think," she said, with an emotional quiver in her voice. A bit more bravely, she walked up and down the piano, more excited with each sound she made. Soon she was running up and down the length of the cloth, leaping and cavorting and snorting. "Oh, listen to that!" she shouted hopefully at one lucky accident. "That sounded a bit Beethoven-y right there, didn't it?"

"Almost," said Hallie.

"No, it did!" said Cassie. "The storm part—listen!" She jumped on a bunch of notes as hard as she could, and it did sound a bit like thunder, but not much like Beethoven. "Yes, that's it!" she said. "I've almost got it!

For the rest of the day she experimented with her new instrument, happier than she'd ever been in her life; happier, probably, than most cows had ever been in theirs.

The happiness lasted three days. Then as she got used to the instrument and it was no longer a novelty, she started to hear what she was doing. Even Cassie had to admit it didn't sound anything like Beethoven and, in fact, very little like music.

But this time she didn't get discouraged.

"I have to have a teacher," she said. "I can't do this on my own."

"Now what?" Myles said after hearing the news.

"Well, we get her a teacher," said Hallie.

"Where?"

"We look around."

"Where?" Myles said, beginning to tire again of inventing Cassie's life.

"Well, Maybe Mr. Katzenbach would like to work with her," David said.

Myles pulled ferociously on his mustache. "Listen," he said. He cleared his throat and sat down, motioning for Hallie to do the same. "I like my life," he said. "I like it the way it is. I don't want a circus around here."

"It will be good for business," Hallie pleaded.

"Business is good enough."

"But . . ." Hallie started. Myles put up a hand.

"I don't want reporters showing up, and I don't want an endless parade of visitors. I like my life just the way it is. We make enough to get by, and we have a bit of peace and quiet. That's more than I can say for most people. I went along with this cow business because it seemed a practical way to get a little milk. It's getting not to be practical. The deal was, the two of you took care of the cow. I'm done with it. I don't have time for any of it."

"But she's not just an ordinary cow! We have a miracle on our hands!"

"You have a miracle on your hands. I said it once, and I don't want to say it again. She's your responsibility. I don't have the time. What's at the end of all of this, I don't know. But if things start getting out of hand with Cassie, we'll just have to let her go. I'm not turning my life over to a cow. No matter how talented she is. I don't want a circus around here."

David gulped hard, but he nodded in agreement. So did Hallie. They knew their father very well, and there would be no arguing this point with him.

The next problem was how to tell Mr. Katzenbach.

"We just tell him," said David, with an easy shrug.

"Tell him what?"

"We tell him we have a talking cow who plays the piano. What else can we do?"

"He wouldn't believe us."

"Maybe it would be better to just bring him over and let him see for himself," Hallie said.

"Why would he want to come here?"

"We can just say we have admired him for a long time and wanted to give him a surprise."

"We'll be giving him a surprise, all right," Hallie said. "We'd better have a chair nearby."

The next day at school they approached Mr. Katzenbach.

"A surprise for me? Why do you have a surprise for

me?" Mr. Katzenbach asked warily, his eyes closing into small slits.

"Well, we admire all your hard work and thought you needed cheering up."

"You find me sad?"

"No, no, very cheerful, but everyone could use more cheer in their lives, don't you think?" Hallie improvised, trying to keep her face from betraying anything at all.

Mr. Katzenbach pursed his lips, anxiously examining their faces to find out what was going on. It was obviously a practical joke. The students didn't like him and he didn't think much of them. Why would they want to cheer him up?

"I have much to do," he offered back. "I am a very busy man. Perhaps I could come over some other day." He made a move toward the door.

"It would be good if it was today," David pleaded, slightly blocking his way. "The surprise is kind of urgent."

"An urgent surprise?" asked Mr. Katzenbach, more suspicious with every moment. "What could be so urgent?"

"You'll see when you get there," Hallie interrupted. "I promise you won't be disappointed."

Mr. Katzenbach's curiosity finally got the better of him, and he relented. That afternoon he showed up promptly at five, grudgingly accepted their offer of tea, and sat stiffly in the living room. He sipped his tea loudly and said nothing. Hallie and David tried to make small talk, but nothing they said interested Mr. Katzenbach. He answered direct questions, but only with a curt yes or no, trailing off into a mumble. When the silence grew unbearable Hallie stood up. "Time for the surprise!" she said cheerily. She and David took Mr. Katzenbach into the backyard. David brought a chair for him, and Hallie wiped it off vigorously before he sat down. Cassie was in her stall, watching expectantly, and when David called to her she got up and lumbered over to her huge piano. David got on the keyboard with her, gave a "one, two, three," and the two of them plowed into a spirited version of "Chopsticks" with David stomping out a simple bass line with his feet. When they finished they looked over at Mr. Katzenbach.

"Well," David said, relieved that it was over, "that was it. This was the surprise."

"Yes," said Hallie. "That was the surprise."

"Interesting," said Mr. Katzenbach. "Quite a phenomenon. What has it to do with me?"

"Cassie needs a teacher and we thought you might be interested," David started to say, and Hallie jumped in urgently.

"She's desperate to get better, and as you can see she's loaded with talent. It's a kind of a miracle, really, when you stop to think about it, and we thought you might want to take her on as a student."

They waited for a response from Mr. Katzenbach. He sat ramrod straight in his chair, not moving a muscle. It seemed as if a week went by. Then he spoke, very quietly.

"You want me to give some piano lessons to your cow?" he said, almost inaudibly.

"We thought it might be kind of fun," David said breezily.

"You thought it might be fun for me to give piano lessons to a cow."

"Yes. We did." David repeated.

Mr. Katzenbach stood up and cleared his throat. "My poor parents," he said slowly in a voice shaking with emotion, "my poor parents scraped and scrimped all their lives so that I should have a musical education. Since I was five years old I studied like a slave. Because you see, in Vienna, it was not like it is here. To get into music school you had to play five instruments. *This was just to get in,* mind you. . . . And I *stayed* in. I studied composition and theory and harmony. I was supposed to be a conductor, you see. I should have been a *conductor,* you understand, but never mind my whole life story. This isn't the time or place. It's enough to say that I am not a conductor. What I am is a teacher of tone-deaf children who can't tell the difference between a bassoon and a harmonica! Children who have no culture, no music, no literature. Isn't it enough I'm in this godforsaken part of the universe with no one to speak to? Isn't that enough? Now I'm supposed to become the instructor of a cow? You think this is the way I should end my days?" Mr. Katzenbach paused, waiting for someone to say something consoling, but neither Hallie nor David could speak.

"Nothing more need be said." Mr. Katzenbach stood up. "I can't believe that I am even having this discussion. Can you hear what it sounds like, what I'm saying? That a human being is even asked such a thing?" He put the teacup down carefully on the chair, bowed a little bow and started to leave. "Thank you for the tea. I think I will not end my days as the instructor of a cow."

"We'll walk you home," Hallie said.

"No, I would like to walk alone," Mr. Katzenbach said quickly. He gave them a feeble wave and left.

"What's wrong?" his wife asked, when he got home. He shrugged, made an ambiguous gesture with two fingers, and went to bed with all his clothes on.

CHAPTER X

HALLIE AND DAVID were undaunted by Mr. Katzenbach's rejection.

"What do we do now?" Hallie asked David after he had gone.

"Call Vivian," David answered without a second's hesitation.

"Does she know how to play the piano?" asked Hallie.

"Vivian knows everything," said David. This time Hallie didn't argue.

They called Vivian and, sure enough, Vivian could play the piano.

"Well, I only studied for a couple of years in my youth," she said on the phone, "but I'm sure I could remember enough to work with a beginner. Who's the student?" she asked brightly.

"Cassie," said Hallie.

"Your cow?" Vivian asked without a hint of shock, as befitted a retired librarian.

"Yes," Hallie answered.

"An interesting challenge," said Vivian.

The next morning Vivian arrived and Cassie demonstrated her stuff. She ran up and down the piano making all sorts of interesting sounds.

"A good beginning," said Vivian, always positive. "She's got a very light touch for a cow." She turned to Hallie and David. "I'll be delighted to teach her the rudiments of music," she said. "I can't take her very far. I know how to read music, but just barely. I know what each note means and I know the time signatures but as far as real technique is concerned, I won't be of much help."

115

"I'll be playing *Beethoven!*" Cassie said in a hushed and worshipful tone, when Vivian had left.

The next day Vivian came back with a stack of cardboard.

Myles was in front of the shop waxing a small bureau. "What have you got there?" he asked, as she marched by.

"Flash cards!" Vivian chirped brightly. "For your cow! Tools from my childhood! I made them up last night!"

She hid the cards behind her back, walked into the yard, and planted herself in front of Cassie. When she had Cassie's full attention she dramatically whipped out a card and held it up in front of Cassie's face. On the card was a single musical note.

"What's that?" Cassie asked suspiciously.

"Middle C!" pronounced Vivian. She walked over to Cassie's piano and stamped aggressively on middle C.

"Hmm," Cassie said, frowning intensely.

Vivian turned over the next card.

"F!" she said. She walked over to the piano again and stepped on the F key. "Try it," she said, and she turned back to the first card. The middle C. Cassie walked over to the piano and pawed the note.

"Fantastic!" said Vivian clapping her hands. "You'll be playing 'Für Elise' before you know it!"

"What's 'Für Elise'?" Cassie asked.

"It's Beethoven! The first Beethoven piece everyone plays. You'll be doing it in no time!"

Cassie's ears went back. "No time? How long is no time?" She asked.

"Oh, two or three months," Vivian said.

"What do you mean, three months?" Cassie said, her ears flattening out on her head.

"I mean, you're so fast that you'll be playing Beethoven in just a few months."

"What will we be doing for three months besides playing Beethoven?"

"Well," said Vivian, "you have to get some basic techniques first. You have to learn all the notes, work your way around the keyboard, study some scales, some easy pieces—that's the way it works."

Cassie snorted, walked over to her pen, and turned her back on everyone.

"What's going on?" David called out. Cassie didn't answer. "What's wrong with you?" he said. "Isn't this what you want? You want to learn how to play the piano? Well, here's your chance."

"No one told me about notes," said Cassie huffily.

"Well, that's the way you do it," said David. "First you learn to read music. You learn the notes, and after that, then you learn Beethoven."

"I don't need to learn music. I need to learn *Beethoven*. Music to me is *Beethoven*! Just get someone to teach me *Beethoven*!"

"No one will do that, Cassie!" Hallie shouted, fed up with Cassie's petulance. "Anyone who knows Beethoven is going to want to hear him played right! And you won't play him right until you learn how to play the *piano*!" There was a no-nonsense streak in Hallie that was just like her father's. When she used a certain tone of voice it was the end of the argument. You didn't cross that line or something terrible would happen. Once she got to that place, you either did what she said or you went away somewhere.

"You win," Cassie said sullenly. She lumbered heavily to her feet.

No one answered.

"I said, you win," she repeated. "I'll do what you want."

"What *we* want?" Hallie asked in disbelief.

"Yes," said Cassie.

"You miss the point," Hallie called out. "It's not what we want. Nobody cares if you play the piano or not. But if someone wants to play the piano there's a way that it's done, and if *you* want to play the piano that's the way you'll do it." Cassie snorted and went back to sulk some more. No one paid any attention. The three of them went into the kitchen for some tea. A few minutes later Cassie popped her head in the window, smiling and cheerful. "Fine!" she said breezily. "Let's go! What's the problem?"

And so the difficult time began. A time very far from Cassie's dreams. A time when she had to focus on tiny things. When the notes become like gnats and flies instead of music. A time for playing scales. Small sections of things. Not songs or pieces. And playing them over and over until she sometimes felt hatred for what she started out loving. For you see, at the beginning of music the mind has to go in two places at the same time. One half is buried in details. In tiny things done over and over again until each little action is perfect and under your control. That's one part of your mind. The other part has to remember what beautiful things sound like. Has to imagine what it's like to soar and glide with an instrument, and trust that someday, when the endless details have been mastered, that your hands will sing and fly and dance almost by themselves.

This was hard for Cassie. She had to be reminded over and over again that at the end of all the scales and memorizing was Beethoven. She had trouble concentrating. Her mind wandered. She got petulant. She grumbled and groused and got bored. She rolled her eyes around in her head every time Vivian asked her to repeat something. She had to learn how to be gentle at the piano. How to float on the keys when doing a scale. How to touch a note with her hoof so lightly that she could hardly feel it. People can do this more easily than cows, as you might imagine, since almost the whole of our body is away from the keyboard. But Cassie had to put her whole weight down on the keys when she played. She had to stand on the piano and *think* lightly. "You're a bird!" Vivian would call out. "You're a big, beautiful bird!"

To Cassie's credit, as time went on she began to become more disciplined. She began to see the small gains she made every few days. Before long she knew the names of the notes and could play all the scales with ease.

One day Vivian came in with some big sheets of newsprint. She held one up in front of Cassie. There were big clumps of notes on each page.

"What's this now?" Cassie asked.

"Try it and see!" Vivian chirped.

Cassie stared at the clumps of notes for a while. "It's a song!" she said when she'd deciphered the notes. "My first song!"

It was a simple piece, written by Vivian, using all the elements of music that Cassie had learned. Cassie jumped right into it, slowly working her way up and down the keyboard while Vivian walked with her on the other side, holding up the music. Within a half an hour she was playing it almost perfectly. "David! Hallie!" she called out. "Listen to this!" David and Hallie came outside, plopped down in the grass and listened as Cassie performed her first piece. It was over in a minute, but at the end of it she was as proud (almost) as if she'd played "Für Elise" by Beethoven.

David and Hallie applauded, showered Cassie with hugs and picked her a bouquet of wildflowers, which she blushingly accepted and then ate. "This is nothing," said Cassie, munching on the stems, flushed with excitement and the success of the moment, "it's only the beginning." The tone in her voice and the look in her eye should have been a warning, but everyone was too excited to notice.

For weeks Vivian put aside her precious artwork and concentrated on writing simple pieces for Cassie. She had to be careful not to write chords with too many notes since Cassie could only play four at a time—human pianists can play up to ten notes at a time if they have to.

Cassie's playing improved so quickly that Vivian's pieces were soon too easy for her, and she had to buy piano music from a store in Sydney. Cassie rarely stopped practicing now. When someone wasn't there to hold the music for her she would improvise little tunes or try to piece together sections from whatever Beethoven she could remember. Beethoven was the hardest, and you could see that her inability to master any of his works was frustrating, only she behaved herself and didn't say anything about it. For a while. In the meantime, Vivian was sore and exhausted from all of the running. Hour after hour she scurried up and down the opposite side of the piano holding up the music for Cassie to read. Because the piano was forty feet long it wasn't possible to use a music stand. She thought about buying roller skates so she wouldn't have to run so much, but they wouldn't have worked on the grass. After one taxing morning she fell to the ground, exhausted. "Too much," she said, panting for breath. "You have to learn this stuff by heart." But then Myles had another brainstorm. He found an old piece of railroad track, made a couple of wooden wheels, attached the music stand to the wheels, and put the whole thing on the track with a rope pulley. Vivian and David stood at far ends of the track and pulled the music stand back and forth, depending on where on the piano Cassie was playing.

"Not the way I thought I'd be ending my days!" Vivian called out cheerily as she hauled the music stand over to her end. "I thought I'd be sorting file cards in the dark somewhere, but here I am; a patron of the arts, and developing biceps, too!"

CHAPTER XI

FOR MANY WEEKS Elaine Katzenbach watched her husband with concern. He was off his feed, and his usual exclamation-point posture had turned into a comma. He drooped. His nose ran perpetually. On weekends he stopped shaving and his usually trim mustache was shorter on one side. He even forgot to clean his eyeglasses. When he didn't get up one Saturday morning his wife tried to take his temperature. "I don't have a fever," he protested, waving her away. He rolled over in bed and stared at the wall. Mrs. Katzenbach watched in concern.

"I'm calling the doctor," she said and started for the phone.

"No doctor!" he called out dramatically. "I don't need a doctor. I'm not sick."

"Well, you are sick," said Mrs. Katzenbach. "Anyone could look at you and see that you're sick. I'm calling the doctor."

"I'm heartsick! Who can help me?"

"What do you mean, 'heartsick'?" She was a no-nonsense woman from the island and she often didn't understand his big-city problems.

"Heartsick!" Mr. Katzenbach repeated. "All my hopes, all my work, my possibilities I have submerged in this small life! A punishment for some horrible crime I committed, although no one tells me what it is! I am trapped in a nightmare! I have been treated like a dishrag for too long! Do you hear me? Too long! It has broken my spirit."

"What happened?" said Mrs. Katzenbach.

"Everything happened! My whole life happened!" Mr. Katzenbach said, sitting up now and shouting to an imaginary audience of a thousand people.

"But what happened recently?" Mrs. Katzenbach said, not impressed with his dramatics.

"Recently? *Recently?* I am living with fish traps and farmers! With no art! No culture! That's what happened to me recently!"

"Did someone do something to you?" Mrs. Katzenbach said, beginning to suspect that he was burying something. Some event that he wasn't talking about. She ran back over the last few weeks in her mind to try to pinpoint the moment when he had started fading. A picture of him moping and grousing after visiting David and Hallie came into her head. "What happened at the Kennedys'?" she asked.

"The Kennedys'?" Mr. Katzenbach asked with not a little irony. "What happened at the Kennedys'? Let me tell you what happened at the Kennedys'. I told them who and what I was! That's what happened at the Kennedys'!"

"What did they do that was so terrible?" Elaine asked. "What did they do that put you in this state for two months?"

"What did they do that was so terrible? What did

they do?" Mr. Katzenbach said. He got out of bed, hiked up his pajamas, and stood as tall as he could make himself. "They asked me if I would teach music to a cow! That's what happened at the Kennedys'!" Mr. Katzenbach marched around the room, some color coming back to his cheeks. Maybe too much.

Mrs. Katzenbach shook her head, not understanding. "What do you mean, they asked you to teach music to a cow? That sounds insane. No one would ask such a thing without being insane."

"I tell you that's what they asked me! They have a cow in the backyard. They took me outside to look at a cow who plays piano, and I am supposed to teach it how to play Beethoven."

"They have a cow who plays the piano?" Mrs. Katzenbach asked incredulously. *"They have a cow who plays the piano?"*

"Yes."

"An ordinary piano?"

"No, no, no!" Mr. Katzenbach shouted peevishly. "How could a cow play an ordinary piano?"

"Well, you said she plays the piano, how am I supposed to know?"

"The cow has a piano that's forty feet long!" Mr. Katzenbach shouted, throwing his arms out wide. "How could a cow play an ordinary piano with those hoofs? Think for a minute what you're saying."

Mrs. Katzenbach looked at her husband as if he were some kind of bug. "You stupid little man," she said quietly. "You had the chance of a lifetime and you threw it away."

"You want me to be a teacher to a cow?" Mr. Katzenbach sputtered.

"A cow who plays the piano!" Mrs. Katzenbach snapped. "Think what that means! You had a chance to be part of something the world has never seen before, and all you could do was get all puffed up. You are a silly little man!"

She went into the kitchen and took out a pie that she'd baked for dinner. "Now here's what you're going to do," she said, holding up the pie. "You're going back there with this pie, and you're going to see if the job is still open. If it is, you're taking it, and you're taking it with no conditions. And no lectures. Do I make myself understood? Do you hear what I am saying?" Mr. Katzenbach nodded yes. She marched to the hall closet, threw him his shirt and pants, and pushed him into the bathroom. When he had dressed she put a cloth over the pie, shoved it into his hands, and pushed him out the door.

Hallie was weeding the backyard when Mr. Katzenbach came by. Vivian and Cassie were looking at the music for an early Mozart sonata. Cassie was staring intently at the large notes, which were clothes-pinned onto the rolling music stand.

"Hello!" Mr. Katzenbach called, waving as he walked briskly past.

Hallie waved back.

"I'm just passing by!" said Mr. Katzenbach.

"That's nice!" Hallie called.

Mr. Katzenbach walked a hundred feet past the house, turned around, and backed up. "Well, now that I'm here, I might as well say hello!" He twisted his mustache and chuckled uncomfortably. He rose up and down on his heels several times, like a bird doing some sort of mating dance.

"Oh, look what I have here," he said. "I have something here. A leftover pie from yesterday. I was taking it to the Kehoes', but now that I'm here . . . maybe you people like pie?"

"Well, yes, we do like pie," said Hallie. "Thank you very much."

"Don't mention it," said Mr. Katzenbach, still raising and lowering his heels. There was an uncomfortable silence.

"Would you like to come in and have a cup of tea?" Hallie asked, to fill in the space.

"I wouldn't mind," said Mr. Katzenbach. They made a move for the kitchen. "How's your cow, by the way?"

"She's good," Hallie said suspiciously.

"I see she's now interested in Mozart," he said, craning his neck to try to get a glimpse of what Cassie was up to.

"Not really," said Hallie. "She puts up with Mozart in order to get to Beethoven."

Mr. Katzenbach's eyebrows shot up into his hair. "She puts up with Mozart," said Mr. Katzenbach, chuckling and shaking his head in disbelief. "An amazing thing," he said. "You don't hear that every day in the week."

"I guess that's true," said Hallie.

"She puts up with Mozart," he said again, a touch

of scorn creeping into his voice. "There are those who think that Mozart was a genius, you know."

"I know," said Hallie.

"And you have a cow who puts up with him."

"Well, Cassie thinks he's flighty."

Mr. Katzenbach nodded slowly, biting his lip to keep himself from saying all the things that were on his mind. Instead he said simply, "Maybe after tea we'll take a look at her, see how she's progressing."

"That will be fine," said Hallie. She put the kettle on and they talked politely about the weather while the water boiled. Hallie cut some pie, gave a piece to Mr. Katzenbach, took a wedge for herself, and poured the tea. They talked some more; about school things, about how good the pie was, about this and that, and after an appropriate time Mr. Katzenbach said, "Well, maybe we'll go and say hello to your cow." He got up from the table and started to walk out the door.

Just as he got to the yard Cassie jumped on the keyboard and into the first chords of her Mozart sonata. The sound threw Mr. Katzenbach back against the house. He thrust his arms out behind him so as not to fall down, and stood transfixed as Cassie went through, for the first time, the difficult and subtle first movement of the sonata. There were mistakes, the interpretation was clunky and ragged, notes were missing; but there was no doubt that Mr. Katzenbach was hearing music.

At the end of the first movement Mr. Katzenbach walked over to Cassie, hardly able to contain himself. "Well!" he said, beaming and rubbing his hands together, "this is another story! This is now *something*! This is no longer a *cow*!" There was more passion in his voice than anyone had ever heard from him. "This is now almost a *musician*!" he went on. "Not a great gift, mind you, not a genius, but with some serious work, we won't have a complete embarrassment on our hands. Congratulations," he said, patting Cassie many times on the back.

"Now let's begin." He rubbed his hands together in a very businesslike manner, walked over to the music stand, took out a pencil, and made some sweeping lines. "Excuse me," he said pushing Vivian to one side. "Here. This is a crescendo," he said, and he made a big < over a group of notes. "Here is obviously a nice, long legato line, here . . . you don't want

132

choppy little notes in here . . . no chicken sounds, do you understand my meaning?" He went on marking up the music.

Vivian looked on, standing straight as a stick, feeling very left out, like a lost little girl, but not wanting to interfere. She had always known that someday Cassie would need a better teacher, and here he was.

At first Cassie felt assaulted by Mr. Katzenbach, but as she concentrated on what he was saying it became clear that the man knew what he was talking about. He knew music, and he knew Mozart. Cassie became like a big sponge, taking in his ideas as fast as he rattled them off. When he finished his comments he asked her to repeat the movement, paying attention to the marks he'd made.

Cassie followed his directions and the piece sounded better than anything she'd ever played. His ideas made the music more exciting. More dangerous. It was as if Mozart were playing a game with the pianist. Sometimes the music soared, sometimes it staggered and almost fell, then came a sweep of chords that picked up the melody just before it collapsed and threw it up in the air. Sometimes the music came to a complete jarring stop, as if the piece were over—and then out of nowhere the notes would jump out of hiding with a crash as if to say, "Only fooling!" Sometimes it was somber and sad in the upper section and playful in the bottom, sometimes the reverse; sometimes the melodies would be stretched till Cassie wanted to scream, "Too slow! Too slow!" Then a rush of notes tumbled out that were almost too fast, creating a wrenching pull and a balance . . . such a delicate balance . . . And so many games in his music! Leapfrog, tug-of-war, tag, hide-and-seek . . . And the melodies! The endless melodies! Mozart kept them going and going and going, sometimes in such long lines that Cassie couldn't follow them, yet they went on and on, pouring and pouring, still coming and coming. . . . Where did such imagination come from? Such endless invention?

Mr. Katzenbach stood ramrod-straight, conducting furiously, a frown between his eyes, but a big tight smile on his mouth. Then it ended in a gentle crash of chords and it was over.

Mr. Katzenbach patted his wet face with a handkerchief.

"So," he said smugly. "That was Mozart. Flighty

Mister Mozart. Flighty Mister boring Mozart."

Cassie stood sweating and panting, her eyes glazed, but feeling happier than she had ever thought possible. Not that she would have admitted it, but she could see that Mr. Katzenbach could be of great help to her. And also that Mozart was not as bad as she had thought. He wasn't Beethoven, of course, but he wasn't bad.

From that moment on, Mr. Katzenbach was Cassie's teacher. No one was asked, there were no agreements, no contracts were signed, not even a handshake, it's just the way it was. Vivian became Mr. Katzenbach's assistant, helping with scale studies and exercises while he was at school. She accepted her new job without any complaint; happy to be needed, and ready to serve in any way that was called for. Hallie watched Vivian carefully, saw how she accepted her new, less important role, without jealousy or anger. And when Hallie saw that Vivian's generosity was real, Hallie completely changed her mind about her. "Underneath all the information Vivian is a pretty nice person," she said to David one afternoon.

"I knew that already," David answered.

Cassie did scale study for hours every morning. Where she got the patience no one knew. Mr. Katzenbach came over after school each day and drilled Cassie with tempo, with phrasing, with interpretation, and if you didn't know, you would think you were hearing army maneuvers instead of music lessons. Mr. Katzenbach turned into a dynamo, his arms flailing wildly, his body language constantly imitating the music. This usually shy little man yelled, jumped, hunched over, tiptoed, crouched, and sprang, calling out all the while: "One! Two! Three! Quiet, here, gently! Now *crescendo!* Don't be afraid! Louder! Louder! Now softly . . . softly . . . creep up on it, creep! Creep! Now legato . . . *legato!* Lightly on the keys! Don't stomp like an elephant!"

At the end of each session Cassie fell in a heap on the ground, bloodshot eyes staring, panting, and frothing at the mouth. The first time Hallie saw her in this state she ran over in a panic. "Are you all right?" she asked.

"Never better," beamed Cassie, gasping for breath.

"It's a good thing the Animal Protection Society

doesn't come by," Hallie said. "If they saw you right now they'd have us all arrested."

In the evenings Mr. Katzenbach spent his time transcribing piano music from ten fingers to four hoofs. Not an easy task. But it filled him with a sense of purpose that he hadn't felt for a long time. "I see a brilliant future for her," he said to Hallie and David. "But don't tell her. It will go to her head."

Myles remained skeptical about the whole business. Something about it made him uncomfortable and he continued to distance himself from Cassie's education. He knew he couldn't keep his children from doing what they needed to do; they would resent him if he tried to stop them. They had to learn their lessons in their own way, but he didn't have to participate. So he went about his business and kept his mouth shut. "Time will tell," he said to himself. "Time will tell."

CHAPTER XII

S PRING CAME and Mr. Katzenbach had to cut back on his time with Cassie.

"Why?" Cassie asked in alarm, worried that her lifeline was going to be cut off.

"Spring concert," said Katzenbach. "I have to earn a living, you know."

They were all sitting around the kitchen table, with Cassie outside, her big head looking in the

138

through the window. "What's 'spring concert?'" she asked.

"Well, you know, it's the concert they have every spring at the high school."

"Who plays?"

"The school orchestra."

"How do you get to be in the school orchestra?"

"You have to go to the school, and you have to play an instrument."

"Hmmm," said Cassie.

Hallie knew that 'hmmm.' "What's on your mind?" she asked warily.

"What?" Cassie asked, pretending she didn't hear.

"You heard me. What was that 'hmmm' all about?"

"I was just thinking maybe that's the way to start."

"Start what?"

"My career, of course."

"By being in the high school orchestra?"

"Yes."

"Well, that would be nice, but you can't play in the orchestra unless you're a student at the high school."

"That would be fine," said Cassie. "I'll do that."

"They won't take you."

"Why not?"

"You know why not."

"Do you mean because I am a *cow*?"

"That's right."

"Are you saying that because I am a cow I have no rights in the community?"

"Oh, you have rights, but I don't think going to high school is one of them."

"Because I am a cow I don't deserve an education. Is that what you're saying?"

"I didn't say anything of the sort. I merely said that cows don't go to high school."

"What you are saying is the cows haven't gone to high school."

"I'm not getting into this," Hallie said, waving away the conversation.

"Listen," said Mr. Katzenbach. "For a change, let's avoid an argument. I will go look in the town statutes and see if there are any rules about cows in high school and such things."

"Don't do it," said Hallie firmly. "I don't care what the statutes say about cows going to school. Just think about what would happen."

"What would happen?" Cassie asked.

"What would happen? Well, for example, do you take a bale of hay in your lunch box or do you join everyone in the school cafeteria? And what toilet do you use? And do you take the school bus? And if so, how many seats do they rip out so you won't be a hazard to yourself and everyone else? And will you have to wear a dress? This is crazy. I'm not getting into it."

"All right, all right," Mr. Katzenbach said. "There's another solution."

"Like what?" Hallie asked.

"She can be the surprise guest soloist. That way she doesn't have to be a student."

Cassie mulled it over. She looked up in the sky, chewed her cud, musing over the sensation she would cause. "I like it," she said finally.

"That's the solution," said Mr. Katzenbach. "That way, she comes only on the evening of the concert itself. I will play piano for the rehearsals."

"Maybe she should play with the orchestra a couple of times so they get used to each other," David said. "If she just shows up at the last minute the orchestra will go crazy."

"Perhaps just the last rehearsal. On the day of the concert," Mr. Katzenbach said.

"It's a small town," said Hallie. "The students have to go home for dinner after the rehearsal. Between dinner and the concert the whole town will know about it."

"Maybe you're right," said Mr. Katzenbach. "Better not to take a chance. I do all the rehearsals, Cassie does the performance."

And it was settled. But what music would she play?

"Beethoven's Sixth Symphony," said Cassie.

"Impossible," said Mr. Katzenbach.

"Why?" Cassie asked.

"Because there's no piano in Beethoven's Sixth Symphony."

"Put a piano in it."

"Just like that? You want me to fix Beethoven?"

"Why not?"

"Fix Beethoven? Even you know better than that. We'll have to change whatever we play anyway."

"Why?"

"Because you have hoofs not fingers. You can only play four notes at a time. At best. That's why. But never

142

mind, I'm telling you right now, we don't make a concerto out of a symphony! Even if we could, no one in the school could learn a whole symphony."

"Then we have to find a short piece by Beethoven for piano and orchestra," said Cassie, clearly not going to be budged.

"There is none," said Mr. Katzenbach.

"None?" said Cassie. "I don't believe it."

"There are no short pieces for piano and orchestra by Beethoven," Mr. Katzenbach said definitively.

"None?" said Cassie, in disbelief. "How many pieces of music did Beethoven write?"

"About five hundred."

And you mean to tell me that in all of them there isn't one short one piece for piano and orchestra?"

"Not one."

"Let's call Vivian," David said, getting up from the table. "Maybe she knows something we don't."

"I tell you there are no short pieces for piano and orchestra by Beethoven!" Mr. Katzenbach shouted, irate that no one respected his knowledge.

"Well, let's just ask Vivian," David said, and he picked up the phone and began dialing.

"Are you going to teach me about classical music now?" Mr. Katzenbach cried. "Have you, too, suddenly become an expert?"

"It can't hurt to make sure," said David.

"Ach!" said Mr. Katzenbach. He threw up his hands, lay down on the couch and began reading the newspaper.

David called Vivian, who was happy to be of use. "We'll check it out on the Internet," she said. "You'd better come over here, though. There's only one phone line and I can either talk to you or the computer." Mr. Katzenbach threw down the paper grudgingly and they all walked over to Vivian's. By the time they got there she had already found pages and pages of material on Beethoven. A few minutes later she found a site that showed everything Beethoven had ever written. "My goodness," she said when she saw the extent of it, "what a list!"

"Do you see anything?" David asked.

"Just a minute," Vivian mumbled, clicking away on the computer keys. "I've got to sort through a million things here. Okay. They've got everything sorted by instruments. So we jump down to his piano music. Here we are," she said after a minute. "Five piano concertos."

"Too long," Mr. Katzenbach said from where he'd plopped himself down on Vivian's couch.

"A lot of solo piano, and a lot of sonatas for violin and piano."

"She must play with the whole orchestra," Mr. Katzenbach shouted from the other room.

"We have some piano quintets."

"That's for one piano and four strings."

"Here we have something. . . ." Vivian said. "Rondo for Piano and Orchestra."

"By who?" asked Mr. Katzenbach.

"Well, Beethoven," said Vivian.

"There is no such piece," said Mr. Katzenbach with authority.

"Well, here it is right here," Vivian said. "Rondo for Piano and Orchestra in B-flat by Ludwig van Beethoven."

"I don't believe it," said Mr. Katzenbach.

"I'm looking at it right here!" said Vivian.

"There is no Rondo for Piano and Orchestra, take it from me."

"Get up from the couch and look at the screen,"

Vivian said, beginning to take offense. "I'm not making this up, you know."

"I'll believe it when I see it," Mr. Katzenbach said indignantly. He walked over to the computer and looked at the screen.

"There it is in black and white!" Vivian said, pointing to the screen.

"Anyone can write words on a list," said Mr. Katzenbach. "I don't see any music."

"Well then, I'd better get you the music, hadn't I?" Vivian said, taking up the challenge.

"How will you do that?" Mr. Katzenbach asked.

"I'll find a music store on the Internet, and if the piece is in print I'll get them to upload it," Vivian said, fuming. Mr. Katzenbach was in her territory now. There was nothing he could say. Either there was such a piece or there wasn't. They went back to David and Hallie's to wait while Vivian made her search.

A half hour later Vivian came stomping through the front door. "Here it is!" she said, gleefully waving a wad of music at everyone. "Rondo for Piano and Orchestra. By Ludwig van Beethoven. There's his name. Right here," she said, tapping the name with authority. Mr. Katzenbach grabbed the music and took it to the kitchen table to pore over the score. He sang each part, stamping his feet, rubbing his head and waving his glasses as if they were a baton. When he got to the last page, he put on his glasses and stood up. "It's Beethoven all right, but it's also no good. That's why no one ever heard of it."

"Who are you to say that it's no good?" Cassie said indignantly, through the window. "It's Beethoven!"

"He wrote five hundred pieces of music!" Mr. Katzenbach said. "How could every one of them be good?"

"He was a genius."

"Yes. He was a genius. "And he wrote four hundred genius pieces. The rest of them were only good. One or two were even not so good. This is one of them."

"I can't listen to this," said Cassie. "Bad Beethoven is better than good everyone else."

"'Bad Beethoven is better than good everyone else!'" Mr. Katzenbach repeated. "Very nice. We'll make a plaque from these words and hang it out in front of Carnegie Hall."

"It's the way I feel," said Cassie.

Mr. Katzenbach went back to the score. "It's also hard to play," he said. "It's short, it's no good, and it's hard to play."

"I don't mind that it's hard, and I don't care that you don't like it. It's short, it's Beethoven, and I have to play Beethoven. That's the whole point of this."

There was no budging Cassie, and there it was. The opportunity was in front of them, they had an orchestra, the music, and the conductor. It was a small local event, and they had a piece that was at least possible, so they settled on the rondo and Cassie knuckled down to some deep and focused work.

In the next weeks the rondo became Cassie's entire life, and before long, the whole family knew it by heart. Whether they liked it or not. Myles kept away from the house as much as he could. Hallie could sense his discomfort, but when she tried to cheer him up it only made things worse. "We'll be set for life, Dad. When this is over we won't have to worry about anything."

"I'm not worrying about anything now," Myles said. He smiled at Hallie when he said it, but there was no happiness in the smile.

• • •

When the time came to discuss the spring concert Mr. Katzenbach told the students about the surprise soloist. "Someone famous?" a girl called out.

"Not yet," Mr. Katzenbach answered, "but after this concert she will be known all over the world, and so will you. But it means learning a very difficult piece of Beethoven's and practicing more than usual. Are you up to the challenge?"

"Sure!" everyone answered, and they rolled up their sleeves and began to tackle the rondo.

Before long, with Mr. Katzenbach pushing them, they could stagger through the rondo. But it was so much work, so many rehearsals, so much other activity curtailed that Mr. Katzenbach finally got called up by the principal. "What's going on, Hans? We have a school to run," he said. "There are other things besides the orchestra, you know."

Mr. Katzenbach smiled a sly smile. "Don't you worry," he said. "After the concert the school will be on the map like no high school in the whole country."

Something in Mr. Katzenbach's tone made the principal believe him.

CHAPTER XIII

THE WEEK BEFORE THE CONCERT Cassie was anxious and irritable. She kept inspecting the condition of her hoofs. She complained about stiffness in her legs. She worried about every twinge and sensation in her joints, and flexed and stretched them continually to make sure they weren't going to cramp up or give out entirely. She soaked her legs in hot water with Epsom salts twice a day and stood looking off in the distance while she checked each twinge to make sure that it wasn't a disease. The days passed like weeks. She had headaches and was sure she was catching pneumonia.

On the afternoon of the concert she demanded to be brushed and combed and shampooed twice. She wanted to wear something around her neck and nothing Hallie and David found satisfied her. Hallie and David ran around looking for pieces of cloth, checking every kind of color and shape, tearing up old clothes and pieces of material from the shop. Finally they settled on a white silk scarf that Vivian had found in a rummage sale. They tied it around Cassie's neck like an ascot, and that seemed to satisfy her.

For weeks Myles debated whether or not he would attend the concert. He had been very quiet about all the goings-on at the house, knowing that there was no stopping the event ahead. But he stayed in the background. Part of him hoped that the concert would be a failure and that would be the end of it. He feared most that she would succeed, and that his children would be swallowed up in her passion. He had always been supportive, encouraging them in all of their hopes and dreams—how could he stop now? But if Cassie succeeded, what would become of their lives?

In the end, he decided that he had to go to the concert. He had to support his children without becoming tangled in Cassie's dreams and fantasies and needs.

The night of the concert came. And the word was out. Posters had been placed all over the island and people were coming from away as far as Port Hawkesbury and Sydney. There was talk everywhere about the surprise soloist, and the sense that something unusual was going to take place.

An hour before the concert Hallie and David got Cassie into the truck and Myles drove then to the school. This time there was no sneaking backstage, because the school didn't have one. Hallie and David stayed with Cassie in the truck through the first half of the concert. They listened to the music out under the stars, but the loud thumping of their hearts made it impossible to concentrate. They waited silently, nervously, wondering what in the world they were doing, and what would happen to their lives after this evening.

The first half of the program took forever. There was an arrangement of English folk songs, a march by Sousa, and a medley of Broadway show tunes. Intermission finally came and the audience left the auditorium to gather in the hallway for some light refreshments. When the people finally cleared out, Hallie and David went through the back doors, climbed onto the stage and rolled out Cassie's keyboard. With Mr. Katzenbach's help they untangled the mass of wires and hooked them up to the amplifier Myles had borrowed for the show.

When the intermission was over, the audience went back to their seats. They saw the amplifier and the two huge speakers now sitting on each side of the stage. The long Mylar keyboard had been stretched out from one end of the stage to the other and the wires all plugged in. A murmur of excitement went through the crowd. What kind of a contraption was this? What did it have to do with Beethoven? Who was the surprise soloist?

Before they could come to any conclusions, the orchestra came back on stage followed by Mr. Katzenbach dressed in his immaculate three-piece heather-green tweed suit and maroon bow tie. Hallie and David opened the door a crack and watched as the audience settled into their seats. When they had quieted down, David put down two planks and walked Cassie out of the truck. They stood quietly at the doors and peeked through.

Mr. Katzenbach got back on the podium. He led the choir in three short songs, and then it was time for the Beethoven.

"This is it," said David, "it's now or never." For once in her life Cassie had nothing to say. Her heart was beating so hard that it felt as if it would bang through her chest. David and Hallie opened the doors and led Cassie into the auditorium and on to the stage.

A murmur of surprise went through the crowd. "A cow?" they heard people whispering. "What's a cow doing in the auditorium?"

Cassie concentrated on trying to stay calm. She placed herself behind her piano, and nodded to Mr. Katzenbach. A nervous laugh went through the crowd. Would the cow actually be playing the piano?

The laugh shook Cassie out of herself. She threw her head up sharply and glared at the audience until there was complete silence. She pawed the ground a couple of times to limber up, snorted once, and nodded to Mr. Katzenbach. Mr. Katzenbach took a deep breath, waved his arms and the piece began.

Cassie leaped on the piano and played the opening notes. To her complete surprise, her legs didn't buckle, she didn't faint, she hit no wrong notes, and played with such strength and surefootedness that she surprised even herself. Now, in this particular piece of music, the piano plays the first passage alone. Four quick, playful bars of solo piano. Then the orchestra is supposed to come in. Nothing happened.

The silence came crashing in on Cassie. She stopped abruptly and looked out desperately at the faces of the musicians. They were staring back at her with their mouths open and their instruments frozen in midair. Everything stopped.

I knew we should have had a rehearsal, Cassie thought to herself in desperation. Mr. Katzenbach coughed into his fist. Still nothing happened. He smacked his baton down hard onto the podium three times to get their attention. The baton snapped, flew halfway across the stage, and hit one of the kettledrums.

"Ladies and gentlemen," Mr. Katzenbach said in a low growl to the orchestra, "shall we play some music?" The students shook themselves out of their shock and picked up their instruments. Mr. Katzenbach nodded to Cassie. Cassie leaped on the piano again and repeated the first four bars, even more surely than she'd played them the first time. This time the orchestra came in when it was supposed to. As the musicians settled into the piece they forced themselves to watch Mr. Katzenbach instead of Cassie. Every time they drifted Mr. Katzenbach shouted, "Look at me! Look at me! Don't look at the cow!" and as the piece went on and they became comfortable, they began to play with a courage and a passion that Mr. Katzenbach had never heard from them before. The music flowed and flowed and the unity between the instruments became so trusting and true that time disappeared, and this diffi-cult piece, which all these people had taken so many weeks to perfect, was now a rushing river of sound completely out of their control. It belonged to itself. There was no stopping it. This river of music carried them where it wanted to go, and their job was to get out of the way. Mr. Katzenbach conducted as if his life depended on it; his eyes bulging out of his head, the sweat jumping off his face, and he sang the melodies at the top of his lungs while the orchestra played on.

Cassie was in another place. Her body played the music, her hoofs danced over the keys, but she watched herself in a daze from some place far away. Who is this playing? she thought. It certainly can't be me! On and on the music went, Beethoven making all the decisions. And so it went, right to the end where the piano and orchestra met; the last notes sounding like bubbling, joyous laughter . . . spilling and spilling and then coming to an abrupt stop. Not a big ending, not triumphant, or dramatic, but perfectly fitting for this sweet, simple piece.

When the music ended Cassie was jolted back into who and where she was. The music seemed to have lasted only for the blink of an eye. Either that or an eternity, she couldn't tell which. There was a moment of silence while the last notes died away. A deafening silence. Cassie had no sense of who she was or of where she was. Sweating and snorting, shocked and dazed, she looked over at Mr. Katzenbach to see if they had really done it. Had they actually played

Beethoven? And in front of an audience? Was this really happening?

Mr. Katzenbach, sweating and disheveled, beamed back at Cassie. He took a handkerchief out of his pocket, wiped his face, turned to the audience, and pointed to Cassie.

The audience broke out into wild and thunderous applause. "Bravo!" they shouted. "Bravo!" over and over again. They stood up and cheered. Someone ran onto the stage with a bouquet of flowers and laid it at Cassie's feet. People took photographs.

The musicians hugged each other, smacked each other on the back, kissed Cassie . . . all of them feeling like heroes. As if they were at the beginning of something big. Something new and important. They joined their families and friends in the audience and crowded around Hallie and David who told their story to anyone who'd listen, repeating the details over and over again. Reporters from the local papers took notes and flashed cameras at Cassie, at Hallie and David, at Mr. Katzenbach. Mary Murphy from the TV station in Sydney pushed her way through the crowd. She'd driven all the way down to the harbor. "I knew this would be something special!" she said. "I had a hunch! I'd like to do an interview right now. Would you mind?"

"Not at all!" was Cassie's breathless response.

Mary called over her crew and shouted questions at Cassie, Hallie, and David over the noise of the crowd. "What do you see next?" she asked. "Where do you go from here?"

"Paris! Rome! London! New York!" Cassie laughed. "The sky is the limit!"

"Why not?" Mary said. Myles stayed nearby talking with his friends but he watched warily at all the fuss being made. He was introduced to Mary Murphy. "You must be so proud of your children! My goodness what they've done here!"

"Yes, I am," Myles said, "and I was proud of them before, too."

"Did you see Roger Demeter?" Mary asked.

"Who's Roger Demeter?" said Cassie.

"Who's Roger Demeter?" Mary laughed. "Why, he's the manager of the Sydney Symphony Orchestra! He's here, and he was enthralled!" She went looking for Demeter who ran over to David and Hallie and introduced himself.

"I won't mince words," he said. "What I saw was phenomenal! If you find it a suitable idea, I'd like to arrange a place in the next concert for Cassie. Would you be interested?"

"Would we be interested?" Mr. Katzenbach sputtered. "Yes! Yes! We'd be interested! Of course we'd be interested!"

Cassie's eyes bulged out of her head. "When would that be? When could I play with the Sydney Symphony?"

"We've had a cancellation. Someone is out sick, so I could possibly arrange it for next week. Would that be convenient?"

"Yes! Why not!"

"Done!" said Demeter.

"Professionals! I'll be playing with professionals!" Cassie said, unable to contain herself, and then her tone changed immediately. "I want to do one of the concertos," she said, immediately confident and secure.

"Well, I'm afraid there won't be time to prepare," said Mr. Katzenbach. "If they want you next week there will not be time. Better to polish what you already know."

The manager turned to Mr. Katzenbach. "How would you like to conduct the orchestra?" he asked casually.

"Excuse me?" Mr. Katzenbach asked, not believing he'd heard right.

"Maybe Cassie would be more comfortable with you conducting the rondo," said Demeter.

Mr. Katzenbach couldn't answer. It was a question he no longer thought anyone would ask. He'd given up hope that this dream would ever come true, and now it was here, and he couldn't speak. He blushed and stammered, looking for the right words, words of gratitude that wouldn't embarrass him, and hoping that when he spoke he wouldn't cry in front of this stranger. Just as he found enough control to speak, Cassie blurted out, "Is there a choice?"

"Well, yes, of course," said the manager. "You could play with our conductor, Vortag Meter Byrling. But I thought you might be more comfortable with your own conductor."

"Byrling!" Cassie cooed, "do you hear that, Hans? I can play with Vortag Byrling! You won't mind, will you, Hans? Just think of what an opportunity it will be. For all of us."

Mr. Katzenbach cleared his throat and pulled himself together. "No, no, it's wonderful," he said. "Of course you must play with Byrling. How can you not? No, you must play with Byrling." And it was settled.

As difficult as the last week had been, this one was worse. Cassie was sure she was coming down with pneumonia. Her heart pounded erratically, she had nightmares, she couldn't sleep, she couldn't eat, she paced, she complained about the piano being out of tune, about the racket being made by the birds . . . nothing was right.

"You're just nervous about the concert," David told her gently.

"Nonsense," Cassie told him curtly. "I'm completely secure about the concert. It's everything else I'm nervous about."

What kept her from losing her mind was the practicing. As long as she was playing the piano she was fine, so she played it all day long. Mr. Katzenbach helped her to use what they learned from their first performance to make the rondo sound even better. The audience at the school had instructed them. Because even though an audience says nothing during the performance, a good musician can feel them, can sense an audience's attentiveness—their enthusiasm, excitement, or restlessness—and this spurs the musician and makes the performance even better.

On the day of the concert Cassie felt really ready. So did Hallie, David, and Mr. Katzenbach.

When they left for Sydney they were all spotless and gleaming. Hallie wore her one good dress. She'd wanted a new one, but it would have meant ordering from a catalogue or a separate trip to Sydney, and there was no time. She held Cassie's bow in her lap so the wind wouldn't mess it up. David wore a suit and insisted on a vest and a bow tie, both of which he borrowed from Mr. Katzenbach, who once again was decked out in his elegant green suit.

Myles didn't join them this time. He said it was because he had too much work to do, but Hallie knew the real reason. When it came time to go he waved them off till they had disappeared down the road, then and went back into the house. The quiet was a relief from the endless practicing, he thought, but at the same time he wondered how much of his family he would still have after this evening was over.

They rode to Sydney in silence. Hallie told herself all the things she would do for her father to make his life easier when she was rich. She would take him to places that he'd talked about and buy him things he'd always wanted but couldn't afford. She knew he'd put up with a lot over the past year, but it would all be worth it, she told herself, and she'd make sure he'd know how grateful she was for his support.

David was excited, but it was over the magic of the evening and all that it held. He enjoyed dressing up and looked forward to being called up on stage, and he wondered what kind of punch there would be at the party and what the hotel was going to be like. Like his father, he was pretty happy the way things were. A new bicycle wouldn't be too bad, he had to admit, if there was money to be made out of this.

Mr. Katzenbach dreamed of conducting an orchestra someday. With or without Cassie. Leading musicians who could hear what he heard and translate it immediately into beautiful sounds. Cassie was busy trying to focus on not being terrified. She ran over the rondo in her mind, redoing the most difficult sections over and over. She tried to keep from thinking of anything past the performance, although once in a while a picture of her on the front page of a magazine would jump into her head, or a headline about how many recordings she was selling.

When they got to Sydney they parked once again near the stage doors. But this time Cassie marched proudly into the auditorium, clattering down the hall, making as much noise as she could to tell everyone that she was there! No sneaking around like the last time.

The orchestra was rehearsing when she came into the hall, but they stopped what they were doing to welcome her. Byrling walked over, beaming. "A great pleasure," he said.

"Thank you, you beautiful man," Cassie said, and she nestled into his shoulder and licked his neck. Byrling blushed and wiped his neck with a handkerchief while the orchestra laughed and applauded.

Byrling put aside the piece they had been rehearsing and pulled out the music for the rondo. "Are you prepared to do a run-through?" he asked Cassie. "Can we play the piece without stopping?" Cassie nodded, and they were off. Cassie played professionally, confidently, and with a lot of fire. The orchestra leaped right into the new piece with gusto and supported Cassie and seemed very much to be enjoying themselves. At the end they laughed joyfully and gave Cassie a good round of applause. Cassie brushed it aside and turned to Byrling. "We'd better do that again," she said with some urgency.

"Excuse me?" Byrling answered, not sure that he had heard correctly.

"I think we can do it better," Cassie said, almost as a warning.

"What seemed to be the problem?" Byrling asked with an amused smile on his face.

"They were a bit slow and much too loud," Cassie said. "We'd better do it again."

Hallie, David, and Mr. Katzenbach tried to make themselves smaller in their seats, wanting to be anywhere but where they were.

Byrling looking slightly shocked, but being a gentleman, said, "Well, it sounded very good to me."

"Too slow and too loud," Cassie insisted. "The audience wants to hear the piano. I'll be what they're coming to see, and the orchestra was overpowering me. Also, I can play it faster than that. And your trumpet players weren't in tune, if you want to know the truth."

"Well," said Byrling, looking for a way to be generous, "in the first place, I think people want to hear all the music, not just the piano, and secondly, the point isn't to see how fast you can play the piece, but to keep the music under control."

Cassie began to fume. "I want to do it again."

"There's no time. We have other things to rehearse."

"Then I'm not going on tonight," Cassie said. She turned dramatically and walked off the stage. A shock ran through the hall. Hallie and David excused themselves and ran off stage to find Cassie while Mr. Katzenbach tried to calm Byrling and the orchestra.

"Listen here," said a trumpet player, "I'll take that kind of talk from Byrling, but I won't take it from a cow."

"I don't know what she's talking about," said the first violinist. "I thought we played that very well."

"Yes," said the second flute, "maybe we're not Montreal, but we're pretty darned good. Who is she to complain about us?"

"She didn't mean it," Mr. Katzenbach said, trying to laugh it off. "She's nervous. She gets crabby when she's nervous. You have to forgive her. This is a new thing for her."

"We all get nervous," said the kettle drummer, "but we try not dump it on each other. We have feelings, too, you know."

Backstage, Hallie found Cassie and pushed her into a dressing room. "What was that all about?" she said. "What's happened to you? I don't know you anymore. You're nasty to everyone all the time."

"I'm a perfectionist," said Cassie.

"No, you're not," said Hallie, "you're a dictator."

"What's wrong with wanting people to do their best?" said Cassie indignantly. "And what am I supposed to do, lie to them? Tell them it was good when they were terrible? I felt mockery in what they were doing. They looked at me as if I was a cow. They weren't taking me or the music seriously."

"That's the conductor's job to decide, not yours," said Hallie. "Just play the piano and leave everyone alone."

"Maybe they'll play better tonight if they feel

guilty," Cassie said. "Maybe they'll work harder."

"You have gone completely crazy," said Hallie. "I don't know what to do with you. And you know if you don't apologize that they might take it out on you during the performance. Did you ever think about that?"

"They wouldn't do that, would they?" said Cassie, turning pale.

"Why not? Why should they try to please you when you're mean and ungrateful?"

Cassie jumped up and started for the stage.

"Where are you going now?" Hallie called.

"I have to stop them before they do anything they'll regret!" Cassie shouted as she ran onto the stage. The orchestra was in the middle of a Mozart divertimento. "I did a terrible thing!" she blurted out. "Forgive me! I'm nervous about tonight, and I took it out on you and . . . I went too far. I went overboard. I hope you understand."

"Forget about it," said Byrling. "It's fine. We forgive you. Now let us get on with the rehearsal, please." Byrling turned away from her and continued with the orchestra.

Cassie waited to see if her apology had any effect.

But they seemed not to notice her. They were engrossed in their playing, and after a minute she left and went backstage.

"It was a good thing you did that," David said, as annoyed with her as he had ever been.

"Maybe it was, maybe it wasn't," said Cassie, glaring at David. "We'll see how well they play tonight."

The performance that night was even better than the one at the school. When it was over there was more cheering and another standing ovation, more flowers for Cassie, and more interviews afterward and a large reception, and Cassie was treated like a star. It was a role she felt very comfortable with. She told everyone her life story and about her love for Beethoven. She even explained Beethoven to some of the musicians and reporters who listened to her as politely as they were able.

After the reception they went to the Holiday Inn for the night. The manager had offered them the Presidential suite to stay in. "This is not an everyday occurrence, as you can imagine. We're honored that you've decided to stay with us," he said as they walked Cassie up the stairs. Cassie smiled and lowered her eyes in a bad imitation of humility. She squeezed through the door and lay down on the rug, where she quickly fell asleep under the admiring gaze of the hotel staff, the concert manager, and a group of well-wishers.

The next morning Hallie and David were woken by Mr. Katzenbach, who came in with the newspaper.

"Look," he bragged, "look here, our picture in the paper! And on the front page!" He held up the paper and showed Cassie her picture. "'Review inside,'" Katzenbach went on. "Here, read it," he said to Hallie. "I'm too excited."

Hallie opened the page to the review and started reading.

BEETHOVEN
LIKE YOU'VE NEVER HEARD HIM!
by Marge Donnelly

Let me start out by saying that the concert last night in the Sydney auditorium was unique. At its center was a performance of Beethoven's rarely heard Rondo in B-flat, and the pianist was a Guernsey cow. Yes, you heard me right, a Guernsey cow. Before you start laughing, let me tell you that she played with more grace and understanding and technique than anyone would have thought humanly (or should I say, bovinely) possible. It was a major debut.

"Did you hear that Cassie?!" Hallie screamed, hardly able to contain herself. "A major debut!" Cassie sat smugly smiling, as happy as anyone had ever seen her. Hallie went on with the review.

Cassie will surely be a favorite in music halls throughout the world. Watching Mr. Hans Katzenbach's trained cow go through her paces was a unique experience. An extraordinary feat of gymnastics. BUT. And I hate to say it . . . but. When we get past the cow's admittedly enormous athletic abilities, past the fact that the cow is actually playing the piano (albeit an electric piano), and playing Beethoven at that, and after marveling at what must have been extraordinary patience on the part of Mr. Katzenbach (and even the cow)—after drinking in all of these facts, when I finally relaxed enough to close my eyes in order to simply listen to the music, what I heard was neither exciting nor inspiring.

Hallie paused, having the distinct feeling that perhaps she shouldn't read any more.

"Go on," Cassie said, not hearing what was coming.

The playing was heavy-handed (or should I say, hooved?) and the solo part simplified so much (to accommodate the cow's four feet) that what was left of Mr. Beethoven, I'm afraid, would have had poor Ludwig screaming and cursing in a language that only the conductor would understand.

"Well, that's enough of that," Hallie said, and she tossed the paper aside.

"No, no, go on," Cassie insisted. "Finish it!"

Hallie, with her heart in her mouth, gathered up the paper again and finished the review.

So, if you're interested in a novelty act, you won't find a better one in all the world than Cassie the classical cow, but if you're interested in Beethoven's piano music, you are better off staying with Arthur Rubinstein.

Cassie sat motionless. A small vacant smile played on her lips. Her eyes blinked rapidly. She took a long, deep breath and then got up lightly; cheerfully. "I'll be right back," she said, and left the room.

"Where are you going?" David called to Cassie. There was no answer, just the thunderous sound of hoofbeats on the stairwell.

David and Hallie jumped up simultaneously and ran out of the room. "The elevator?" David shouted to Hallie.

"No time!" Hallie called back as she made a beeline for the stairs. "Cassie! Don't do anything stupid!" she shouted as she flew down the stairs, hanging on to the railing for dear life.

Cassie crashed into the lobby and skidded over to the front desk. Gathering herself together, but breathing hard, she smiled pleasantly at the young woman behind the desk. "Could you direct me to the offices of

The Daily Chronicle?" she said as calmly as she was able.

"Certainly!" the young woman answered, brightly. "Left out of the building, two blocks down, make a quick right, and you're there."

"Thank you," chirped Cassie and she raced out the front door, with Hallie following and David huffing and puffing half a block behind.

"Wait up!" David called, but Hallie raced on without looking back. By the time Hallie and David caught up to her she was in the *Chronicle* building. She had just spoken to the guard at the front door and was galloping up the stairs.

"Wait up!" Hallie shouted. When she got up to the second floor Cassie made a beeline for the office that said ARTS AND ENTERTAINMENT. A gray-haired woman with reading glasses on a long metal chain was putting things into a filing cabinet.

"Are you Marge Donnelly?" Cassie bellowed.

"No, I'm only a secretary," the woman said, backing up and holding her heart in alarm.

"Where is Marge Donnelly?" Cassie demanded, trying to smile pleasantly, though the fire in her eyes and her heavy breathing turned the smile into a grimace.

175

"I'm afraid she's not in today," the secretary said, backing into a corner.

"Where can I find her?" said Cassie. "It's a personal matter of extreme urgency."

"She's at her china shop," said the secretary. "This is only a part-time job for her."

"And where would the china shop be?" Cassie asked.

"Around the corner to the right," said the secretary, and the minute she said it she had the feeling that she'd probably made a mistake.

Cassie turned and raced out of the room, down the stairs, out the building, and skidded around the corner, almost colliding with a mailman on a bicycle. "Pardon me," the mailman said. Cassie didn't answer. She was busy looking at store signs. Marge's China Shop was halfway down the block. Cassie plowed through the door.

Marge Donnelly was holding up a flower vase for an elderly gentleman. As Cassie came barreling into the store Marge went pale and her life flashed before her eyes. Somewhere deep down inside, she had known that this was eventually going to happen. All her years as a critic something had told her "Be careful, don't go too far! Someday a crazed musician will come after you! They'll take your review as a personal attack and not as constructive criticism!" And now, here was that musician standing in front of her. And it was a 1,500-pound cow.

"Marge Donnelly?" Cassie bellowed.

"Yes?" said Marge in the bravest and tiniest of voices.

"Marge Donnelly?"

"Yes," Marge answered almost inaudibly.

"You stupid woman!" snarled Cassie, nostrils flaring and flecks of foam at the corners of her mouth. "Last night you were in the presence of greatness! You were witness to the birth of a great artist, and what did you do? You threw garbage at it! What I accomplished in one year no ordinary musician has ever done in ten!"

"Well, there was Mozart," said Marge, in a trembling voice.

"Don't you dare speak to me about Mozart!" Cassie shouted, inching toward Marge and knocking over a half dozen dinner plates with her wildly swishing tail. "I *play* Mozart. What do you do? You sell dinner plates! You . . . you . . . you . . . *critic*! You trample on everything beautiful and valuable! How dare you speak about Mozart! Don't tell me about Mozart! I am intimately acquainted with Mr. Mozart! I don't need you to give me lessons on Mozart, or anyone else!"

"I'm . . . I'm sorry if I offended you. . . ." Marge stammered. "It was only my personal opinion." Her face was pale and her lips quivered. The customer put down the vase, raced past Cassie, and knocked over a bric-a-brac shelf filled with porcelain figurines of children in lederhosen as he raced out the door.

Marge made a move to save her plates, but thought better of it. She backed up out of harm's way.

Cassie plowed on toward her, sending porcelain flying right and left as she fumed down the narrow aisle.

Marge, trapped by the cash register, grabbed a flower vase and held it to her chest as if it was some kind of amulet that would protect her. "I have a right to my opinion," she said as Cassie moved in on her. "It's my duty to report what I see and hear and feel. I owe it to the audience. I can't just say what's expected of me. I'm not hired to make people happy."

"Well, you're certainly not making *me* happy!" Cassie bellowed. "And you're not going to make the audiences happy either, if my ears tell me anything.

Did you hear the way they applauded? It was like thunder! Did you hear it?"

Marge nodded fearfully.

"Well, what was that? Do you think I fooled everyone, or do you think the audience was just stupid? They loved me, you foolish woman! They loved me!"

"What about Beethoven?" Marge asked quietly.

"Excuse me?" Cassie bellowed.

"What about Beethoven?" Marge said again. "Did they love Beethoven, too? Or just you?"

"I—I—let me tell you something!" Cassie sputtered. She tried to answer but words wouldn't come out. Just then, Hallie, David, and two policemen came rushing into the shop.

"Cassie!" Hallie shouted. "Calm yourself now, let's get out of here."

The policemen got between Cassie and Marge and took out his nightstick. They smacked them into their hands a few times, slowing Cassie enough so that she allowed Hallie and David to back her up out of the shop. They petted her and soothed her and slowly got her into the waiting pickup truck.

Mr. Katzenbach apologized to Marge and told her to

total the damages and that he'd send her the money as soon as he got home. Marge said that would be fine, and the agreement seemed to satisfy the police. They told Mr. Katzenbach to take the cow home, but only after they both got autographs. Their wives had been at the concert and had been very impressed. Hallie and David gave them their autographs and got Cassie to put a hoof print on a piece of paper. Her heart wasn't in it, but she thought it was probably better than a jail sentence.

The ride back was quiet. Mr. Katzenbach and Hallie and David contemplated their future, while Cassie lay morosely in the back, trying to make sense of everything that had happened. In the past twenty-four hours she'd been bounced around like a Ping-Pong ball. It was all so complicated that she couldn't figure out how it had all begun. All she knew was that she needed to rest. Marge Donnelly's review reverberated in her brain. And worse than the review was her saying, "What about Beethoven? Did they love Beethoven, too, or just you?" She tried to find an answer to that question; something she could have hurled back at Marge, but nothing came to her.

Back at the house Mr. Katzenbach said his goodbyes, and Hallie and David went inside to tell Myles all about what happened. He listened attentively to all their adventures, but he wasn't surprised and never said "I told you so."

For the next few days the phone didn't stop ringing. Reporters wanted interviews. TV stations wanted Cassie to do appearances. Agents wanted to sign her and cities all over the country wanted her to perform, but Cassie would speak to no one. "The interest will go away," Hallie pleaded. "People will forget!"

"Leave it alone, now, Hallie," Myles said, and finally he just took the phone out of the wall.

In frustration Hallie went to Cassie. "What's happening to you?" she demanded.

"She was right," Cassie said.

"What do you mean, she was right?" Hallie said dumbfounded. "One stupid review and all of your hopes and dreams fly out the window? Where's your famous courage? And what would your Beethoven have done? I'm sure he got plenty of bad reviews."

"They were applauding a cow playing Beethoven," said Cassie.

"Yes? So?" said Hallie, missing the point.

"It's over. I'm done playing," was all Cassie said.

Hallie couldn't believe what she was hearing. "What about all our plans? Seeing the world? Meeting people? What about all that? What about fame and fortune?"

"I'm done with all that," said Cassie. Hallie waited for her to change her mind, to say something further, but Cassie lay down in her stall, turned to the wall, and went to sleep.

CHAPTER XIV

THE NEXT DAY David went to see Cassie. He sat next to her on the ground. "I think you should do whatever you want," he said, caressing her big neck. "I don't care if you play the piano or not. It makes no difference to me. I'll love you either way."

Cassie burst into tears.

"What is it?" asked David.

"I've wronged everyone," she said. "I failed everyone. Mainly Beethoven."

"How did you do that?" David asked.

"I'm not sure," Cassie said.

"Don't worry about it," said David.

"Well, I do worry about it," Cassie said. "I don't know what got into me. How did all this start?"

"Beethoven's Sixth Symphony," said David.

Cassie sighed a long sigh and tried to pull herself together. "Loving Beethoven was a good thing. *Is* a good thing. I thought playing his music would make me like him. When I played his music I felt as if I was him. So courageous. Courageous and open and big. The problem was when the music stopped . . . I couldn't stay like him when the music stopped." She shook her head slowly, sadly. "That was the hard part. But you have to do it. Otherwise the music has no meaning. Beethoven has no meaning. That's why he's in our lives, I think. To point us to our own courage. He's there to tell us what we have to be like."

"Maybe he wasn't like that either," said David.

"What do you mean?" Cassie asked.

"Well, Mr. Katzenbach said he could be pretty mean."

"No," said Cassie, aghast. "I can't believe it."

"That's what Mr. Katzenbach said."

Cassie let that possibility sink in. "Maybe he couldn't be like his music, either," she said.

"Maybe not," said David.

"But then he had a lot to live up to, didn't he?" Cassie said. She tossed her head. "Well, I love him anyway. Whatever he was."

"Maybe that's enough," said David.

"Maybe so," said Cassie. She looked out over hills in the distance and watched the clouds at play in the sky. "Be brave, brave, brave," she murmured, "be brave . . . and joyous."

"Sounds pretty good to me," said David.

Cassie stopped speaking after that. It was as if her reason for speaking had been for one purpose only, and once that purpose had been fulfilled, there was nothing left for her to say. Cassie became a cow again, content to wander around the backyard, chewing her cud and giving milk. She still poked her head in the kitchen window at mealtimes, happy to have her nose scratched, but the music was gone.

• • •

One late afternoon in the early fall, Myles went out to Cassie's shed to nail on a piece of tin for her roof. Cassie tugged at his jacket.

"What is it, Cassie?" Myles asked.

Cassie moved over to her piano, which was rolled up and stuck into a shelf in her shed. She prodded it with her nose.

"Do you want your piano?" Myles asked.

Cassie nodded.

Myles took the piano off the shelf, put it into the yard and unrolled it. He hooked up the wires to the amplifier and went back to the store. Cassie ignored it, seeming to find comfort in its being near, but not wanting to deal with it. It stayed there for a long time. Then one day she began pawing at it gently. She circled her piano a few times, then, tentatively, she touched a few notes with her nose. By the time Hallie and David came back from school she was playing the somber, slow movement from the *Moonlight* sonata.

"Oh, no," Hallie whispered, "here we go again."

David didn't answer. He was listening to Cassie's playing.

It sounded different. It was less showy, less impressive, but it seemed to have more depth. For the first time David was not listening to a cow playing Beethoven. He was just hearing music. And Cassie seemed to be simply there with the music, not trying to be Beethoven. Cassie came to the end of the piece and she stood there, head down, lost in the beautiful silence that sometimes follows a great piece of music.

David thought about telling her how good she sounded, but then he decided not to break the silence. So he just watched her as she walked away from the piano and stood munching on grass, watching the sun as it set over the distant hills. She seemed serene and relaxed and detached.

She played every day from then on, for about an hour or so in the afternoon. It didn't matter whether anyone was there to listen or not. She was just as pleased to do it for the family or their friends, for the wind or the trees, or for no one at all. She discovered her love for the music again, and she didn't need anyone to tell her how good it was, or how well it compared with some-one else's version. She didn't need applause or even an audience. When she played now it engulfed her in a new way. It was the notes. The music itself. It was alive in her in a deep place and she was content.

Cassie was so engrossed now when she played that she didn't notice when Gordon, the MacMannuses' sheep from next door, jumped his fence to listen to her. She didn't notice when he chewed through her fence to get closer to the music, nor how a tear fell from his cheek the first time he heard her play the *Moonlight* sonata. Cassie only noticed Gordon the day he began scratching out bass and treble clefs in the dirt with a stick in his mouth, writing down notes as fast as he could, humming intensely to himself as he went along.